JAMES LEE BURKE
TWO FOR TEXAS

PHOENIX

A PHOENIX PAPERBACK

First published in Great Britain in 1997
by Phoenix
This paperback edition published in 1999
by Orion Books Ltd,
Orion House, 5 Upper St Martin's Lane,
London WC2H 9EA

Reissued in Phoenix paperback 2004

Copyright © 1989 James Lee Burke

5 7 9 10 8 6 4

The right of James Lee Burke to be identified as the author of
this work has been asserted by him in accordance with the
Copyright, Designs and Patents Act 1988.

A CIP catalogue record for this book
is available from the British Library.

ISBN-13 978-0-7528-2135-0
ISBN-10 0-7528-2135-4

Printed and bound in Great Britain by
Clays Ltd, St Ives plc

The Orion Publishing Group's policy is to use papers that
are natural, renewable and recyclable products and
made from wood grown in sustainable forests. The logging
and manufacturing processes are expected to conform to
the environmental regulations of the country of origin.

www.orionbooks.co.uk

TWO FOR TEXAS

ONE

The first day that Son Holland arrived in the penal camp, manacled inside a mule-drawn wagon with seven other convicts, he knew that he would eventually escape, that he would die before he would spend ten years in a steaming swamp under the guns and horse quirts of malarial Frenchmen with Negro blood in their veins and a degenerate corruption in their hearts. But he was just barely nineteen then, still sufficiently naive to believe that his will alone was enough to win his freedom. He didn't know that almost two years would pass before his escape would come almost by accident, and that he would have to help murder a man to accomplish it.

The penal camp was built on a mudflat of the Mississippi River, where it made a wide bend north of Baton Rouge, and at sunset, while he stood exhausted and silent in front of his pen, waiting for the long chain to be slipped free from the iron ring manacled to one ankle, he looked out over the miles of swampland that one day he would have to cross to reach the Sabine River and Texas. White cranes flew low over the dead cypress tops in the sun's afterglow, their wings covered with scarlet, and the willow trees along the banks seemed wilted in the damp heat; just as the pen door was bolted and locked behind him and he lay down on the wood plank in the collective smell of himself and the other convicts, he saw the mosquitoes begin to lift in gray clouds out of the cattails.

Sleep came to him only in the late hours of the night, because the men who were to be whipped for breaking a rule during the day were always taken from the pens after the guards had eaten supper and started in on the barrel of whiskey they kept locked up with the axes and saws. So a man never knew until very late whether he would be called out from the pen, told to pull his cotton breeches over his buttocks and kneel across a log, like a child saying his prayers, and be whipped until he cried and the urine ran down his thighs.

Also, there were the sounds of the convicts in the *maisons de chiens*, the dog houses, a row of wooden boxes where the bad ones were locked in with a hole the size of a cigar for air. There wasn't enough room for a man to sit upright, and after a day his body felt as though he had been turned on a medieval rack; a second day reduced him to a pleading thing that whimpered inside the wooden frame of his agony, while the lines of men clanked past him on their long chain into the marsh. If he was left in there three days, he usually had to be dragged from the box like a dog that had been crushed across the rib cage by a wagon wheel. He would lie in the dirt, his head touching his knees in an embryonic position, his eyes blind to the white sun, his lips caked with his own salt and his eyes absolutely mad.

Son Holland experimented with different ways of getting into sleep, of sinking down past the suck of air behind the horse quirt and the fingernails scratching inside the dog houses. Sometimes he thought about women, but more often in the hot darkness he thought about his home in the Cumberland Mountains of eastern Tennessee. In the center of his mind he could see the dark green of the mountain crests rising out of the morning mist, and as the sun grew hotter and burned away the fog from the river, he saw the dogwood in bloom against the hillsides and the rolling stands of maple and beech trees and yellow birches. But if he dwelt too long upon that vision he would remember the burned cabin and finding his mother and father in the horse lot after the hogs had gotten to them. The high sheriff said it was done by drunk Shawnees, because only a drunk Indian killed like that and did those kinds of things to a man before he died.

Then there was the long ride on the swaybacked chestnut to Memphis, where he sold it for the passage down the Mississippi to New Orleans, that leftover piece of Europe where men who couldn't even speak English made fortunes in the cotton exchange. Then he would feel an anger and shame at his stupidity in thinking that he would be considered anything more as a mountain person than the poor white trash that filtered into the city from the Mississippi River bottoms.

When he entered a public house to eat and was told to go around to the side door by a Negro servant, he backed out into the cobbled street unable to speak and was almost run down by a carriage. He learned quickly that there were only certain places where he entered the front door, and the men seated at the tables were a foul lot who slurped at their tankards of wine and smelled of cured alligator hides and the stagnant water of the marshes. Their skin was discolored a pale greenish cast, because they lived along the bayous or came out only at night to rob from the flatboats on the river, and they all carried razor blades or knives in their beaded moccasin leggings.

He was sleeping on a pallet among the same type of men behind the slave quarters, when he was arrested and put into manacles by two city constables.

Neither of them spoke English, and when he backed away, protesting, "What for? What for? I ain't done nothing," they pressed his hands together, almost gently, and locked the manacles on his wrists. He felt the chain come tight between his clenched fists. A rage swelled in his chest and he swung the loop of chain into a constable's face.

"Don't fight back with them Frenchies, boy," a man on the ground said. "They'll salt your hide when they get you in jail."

The second constable hit him across the ear with his pistol barrel; Son heard the blood roar in his head and he tipped sideways on one foot as though his body were made of wood. He got to his hands and knees, his ear burning, and saw the mud-flecked boot flick out toward his face; then he knew that pain was only a brief thing, a tearing along the jawbone someplace, a glass splinter in the softness of the brain, and finally just a rolling over like a lover into the arms of one's tormentor.

He awoke on the floor of the jail wagon on the way to the city prison, and the constable who had kicked him was sitting on the wooden bench next to the barred door, his small face an indifferent white oval in the moonlight. Son could feel the metal-banded wheels vibrate on the cobbles through the floor of the wagon.

"What for?" he said. The inside of his jaw felt swollen against his teeth, and he wiped a clot of blood off his bottom lip. ·

The constable crossed his leg on his knees and looked out through the barred door.

"What for, you shithog? I ain't done nothing except sleep in the same place as them pirates down there. I don't have nothing to do with where they go at night."

The constable made a motion with his two fingers, as though he were snipping at something with a pair of scissors.

"That don't make no sense."

The constable wet his lips and hummed a sound in his throat, then clipped at the air again and said, in his bad accent, "Cutpurse."

"What?" The word was unbelievable to him, something apart and away from him.

"Cutpurse."

"You're a liar," he said, and looked up from the floor and felt his heart beating.

* * *

"Cutpurse ain't nothing," Hugh Allison said from the bunk next to Son. "That's no bad mark against a man. I was up in front of the same judge three times for the same thing. The only reason he give you them ten years was because you stole it from a quadroon woman that belonged to a gentleman. That's the way the law works with these Frenchies."

I didn't steal it. She lied in the court, with her hand on the Bible, in front of God and all them people, and she looked straight at my face when she lied.

The false dawn had just started to spread in a low gray band across the horizon, dimly outlining the mudflats and the moss in the cypress trees and oaks on the far side of the Mississippi's dark expanse. It was still cool, with a fresh breeze off the water, and mockingbirds swept low over the willows and cattails after insects. Somewhere back in the sandy bottoms of the marsh Son heard a bull alligator roaring for its mate.

"What I mean is, you just stole from the wrong high-yellow woman," Hugh said. "You wouldn't have got all that bad time if you'd taken it from some darky woman down in the market. You just ain't supposed to mess with them gentlemen's quadroons. That's a rule they got down here."

She lied because she left her purse in another white man's home, he thought. The lawyer told me in the jail that you can make a liar of her in front of the court, that you can even suggest she's not a white woman and hence is capable of receiving the insult, but you can never accuse the other gentleman, who is seated next to the cuckold, of lying at the same time, or otherwise they will make sure that you never reach the penitentiary. Don't you understand that, Holland? It's their strange conception of honor.

"You got to stop grieving on it, boy," Hugh said. "You might not believe this now, but one day you'll be out of here. It ain't that way with me. I been in here twice before, and with all that time they give me for killing that fellow, I might get buried here. They'll just dig a hole back in the swamp and drop me in it."

"Hush up, Hugh."

Hugh Allison's skin was sunburned almost black, and his bleached hair was shot through with gray and hung over his head like a tangle of snakes. He had a dozen scars on his body from knife and pistol wounds, and there was a large raised welt above his collarbone where an arrowhead lay embedded under the skin. He was almost blind in one eye, and the pupil stared coldly out of his face like a black marble. He claimed to have been a member of the Harpe gang on the Natchez Trace years ago, and said that he was there when the posse sawed Micajah Harpe's living head from his shoulders.

"You ought to listen to an older man," he said. "There's only one rule to living in here. You take your opportunities."

"What are you saying?"

"You been in the dog box three times, each time for running when you didn't have no chance of getting away. The next time they lock you in there they're going to leave you until your brains melt and run out your ears."

Son looked out through the bars of the pen at the mist rising off the river and the light swelling into the sky. The moon was still hardly visible in the dark blueness of the west.

"I can't make ten years," he said.

"You don't listen, do you, boy? How do you think I lived all these years? There's been many a man that tried to put me under—Indians, redcoats, high sheriffs, these Frenchy guards—and I always come out ahead of them. Because you learn to fight like an Indian. You shoot from behind a tree. You don't fight the other man on his ground."

"I want to sleep," another man said from his bunk.

"Don't that make sense to you?" Hugh said. His cold black eye was wide in the half-light. "One of these days you'll get your chance. Maybe both of us will."

"Did you ever try to run?"

"Hell, yes, I did, and I done it just like you. We was felling cypress about five miles north of here, and Landry let me go into the bushes to take a shit and I kept right on a-going. I didn't make a quarter mile before they run me down. They put me in the dog box for three days. The hinges on the inside was so hot they scalded my hands. I don't remember nothing after the second day. When they took me out my head and my knees was full of splinters."

"Be quiet and let us sleep in the time we got left," the man in the next bunk said.

"Bother me again and you'll be sleeping with my fist upside your head," Hugh said.

At the far end of the camp the door opened on the log building where the guards slept, and Son saw Emile Landry framed in the light from the lantern on the table inside. He wore soiled gray pantaloons tucked inside his boots, a split-tailed coat, and a short stovepipe hat; and in his hands he carried the horse quirt that was weighted in the handle with lead. His brother Alcide Landry stepped out of the log building behind him. They were ten years apart in age, but they could have been twins. Their torsos were unnaturally large for the rest of their bodies, the shoulders an axe-handle wide, and they seemed to have no necks below their small cannonball heads. No one knew where they came from or what they had been before they became guards in the camp. Even the oldest prisoners said the Landrys had always been there. Occasion-ally, one of them would take the riverboat down to New Orleans, but otherwise they lived almost the same life as their prisoners.

Son watched the older one, Emile, walk to the iron bell that hung on the oak tree by the row of pens. He rang the clapper three times, then unbolted the pen where the trusties slept. The trusties filed out in their dirty, blue-striped uniforms and began stoking the glowing ash in the stone oven where all the camp food was cooked. They put one block of cornbread in each wooden bowl and poured molasses over it out of a crock that was swarming with flies.

Emile Landry opened the food slit to Son's pen and let the trusty push in eight bowls and a single pan of water with a cup floating in it.

"Bayou Benoit today," he said, and walked behind the trusty to the next pen. The low clouds on the horizon had turned to pools of fire.

"Oh shit, that's where all that quicksand's at," a man said.

"It ain't no worse than where we was yesterday," another man said.

"You ain't been up there. We cut that bayou three years ago. A whole chain got stuck in it. They was fighting in the water and tearing at willow branches, and by the time Landry come back with a mule and a rope, every one of them was drowned."

"Shut up," Hugh said. "Them men got drowned because they was scared before they went in there."

"And you ain't?" the other prisoner said.

"Not of no Louisiana mud. Just of the dumb sonofabitch that might be on the chain next to me," he said.

Emile Landry came back to the pen with the trusty and unbolted the door. The brass butt of his pistol hung out of his coat pocket.

"Man number one on the stump," the trusty said.

One at a time they stepped out of the pen onto a sawed cypress stump, and the trusty ran the chain through the iron ring banded on their ankles as though he were threading fish on a stringer. The water barrels, the canvas sacks of smoked carp for lunch, and the axes and saws were loaded on the mules, while the men stood silently in the purple dawn. Then the trusties brought up the saddled horses for the guards, and the chains of men filed past the dog boxes, each man in step with the other, behind the switching tail of Emile Landry's mare.

They crossed Bayou Benoit on the chain, the brown water swirling around their chests, and each man's heart clicked inside him as he waited for the moment he could grab for one of the limbs and pull his weight out of the water. The convict in front of Son was an eighteen-year-old blond boy from Natchez, with thick white scars from the guard's quirt up and down his spine. He grabbed onto a willow branch with both hands and lifted himself violently out of the water. A three-foot moccasin that had been coiled on the limb above exploded out of the shadows like a piece of black electricity, its white mouth open wide, and sank its teeth into the boy's throat. He slapped at the writhing snake with his hands, his eyes bulging with shock and terror, and screamed, "Oh God, I am killed."

Son caught the moccasin behind the head and squeezed until the jaws opened and the fangs came loose from the boy's throat, then threw it downstream as far as he could. The boy fell backward into the water on his buttocks and his head went under as though he were resting for a moment, and Son had to grab him under the arms and pull him onto the mudbank.

"Get some wet chewing tobacco on it, Mr. Landry," Son shouted up at the guard on horseback.

"*Il est mort*," Landry said.

"No, he ain't. My uncle back in Tennessee got hit in the face with a copperhead, and we bled him and kept tobacco juice on it, and it sucked that poison right out of there."

The guard motioned to two trusties with his quirt, and they unlocked the bolt on the head of the chain and slid it through the ring on the boy's ankle. The gashes in his throat were turning blue, and his eyes were dilated and shot with blood.

"*La-bas*," Landry said.

The trusties carried the boy between them back on the sandy flat and laid him at the edge of the canebrake. Son waited for something else to happen, but it didn't. The other men were taken off the chain, the trusties went to unloading the mules, and Emile Landry looked first at his pocket watch, then squinted upward at the sun with his small, round face.

"Ain't you going to try to save him?" It wasn't even a direct question, just a simple statement of incredulity.

The guard walked his horse back into the shade, removed his short stovepipe hat, wiped his hand along the sunburned line of his brow, then pinched the hat down on his cannonball head again.

"I'll suck it out myself, Mr. Landry."

"Shut up, Son," Hugh said quietly behind him.

The men filed past the mules and picked up their axes and saws and went to work on the cypress trees along the bayou's bank. In the dappled light of the canebrake Son could see a white foam forming at the corners of the boy's mouth.

"You murdering sonofabitch," he said.

He heard the horse quirt suck through the air behind him, and in the edge of his vision he saw Alcide Landry's livid face just as the weighted handle ripped across his ear and sent him sprawling in the sand. He rose to his knees, his mind roaring with light and sound, the blood already running down into his striped jumper, and then Alcide Landry's boot came up so hard between his buttocks that he thought he was going to urinate.

They chained his hands around a tree for the rest of the day, and gave him a single cup of water while the others ate lunch. The boy died alone that afternoon. Son looked over at him in the growing shadows, at the flies buzzing around his eyes and caked mouth, and for a moment he thought he saw his own face on the boy's.

That night at the camp he knelt over the log, his filthy cotton breeches pulled down to his knees, while Emile Landry whipped the quirt across the white skin fifteen times. Then the trusties carried him trembling to the dog box.

It was a soft, lilac evening when they opened the lid and walked him to his bunk. He couldn't straighten his legs, and his knees caved each time he tried to set his full weight down. The late sun was a red flame through the mauve-colored trees across the river. When they dropped him on his bunk and bolted the pen door behind him, he thought he heard the rumble of dry thunder beyond the horizon.

It was raining softly when he awoke in the morning and the wind from the river blew the mist inside the pen. He knew it was Sunday because it was already past the time when the work gangs should have been deep into the marsh. He straightened his back against the hard boards of the bunk and felt the pain of the dog box slip along his spine and make his groin go weak.

"He really laid the quirt on you, didn't he?" Hugh said.

"He warms to his work."

"You look like they baked you in a skillet. Drink some of this coffee and stretch out your stomach. The worst thing in that box is not having no water in you. You get so damn thirsty in there you drink what little they give you all at once, and then piss it out in your pants. When you try to space out your sips, you watch it steam away in the heat. They know how to make a man work against himself. I heered the French got a prison island off South America somewhere that's so bad nobody believes it till they get there."

Son drank his coffee slowly and sucked on the boiled beans at the bottom of the cup.

"I got a treat for you. Take a chew of this," Hugh said, and handed him a dark twist of tobacco. "That ought to make you right again. I take care of you, don't I?"

"Where'd you get it?"

"Last night a whiskey trader come upriver to see the Landrys and they all got drunk and had a big time shooting at an alligator out on a sandbar. Before the trader left I called him over to the pen and gave him a mouth harp for the tobacco and two cups of whiskey that liked to fried my hair. When I woke up this morning I thought I had broken glass inside me. I never thought whiskey could be that bad. That trader must put dead animals in his still or something."

"You ain't got a mouth harp."

"Well, it wasn't mine but the fellow who owned it couldn't play it worth a shit, anyway."

"Hugh, you better stop getting people mad at you in here."

"What are they going to do? Kick me out of here and send me back to New Orleans?"

Son couldn't help laughing, although the movement sent a shudder of pain down his back again.

"Today we're going to wash our clothes and bathe in the river and take an afternoon nap like gentlemen," Hugh said. "Tomorrow your body won't have no memory of that box. But this time you listen to me. You don't go up against them people again when they got it all on their side. What you done was plumb stupid. Landry wanted that boy to die. Every one of us he don't have to feed means money in his purse to spend on whores in New Orleans."

"You don't let a man die like that."

"Where do you think you are? The regular rules don't have nothing to do with this place. I ain't even going to talk with you about it anymore. You don't learn nothing even when it hits you alongside the head."

There was a crack of lightning across the sky, and the rain began to fall harder, dimpling the wide sweep of the Mississippi. A trusty ran from the log house toward their pen with a set of wrist manacles in his hands, the three-foot loop of chain swinging against his body, his head bent against the rain. He unbolted the door and stepped inside the pen, the water sluicing off his straw hat. He coughed up phlegm and spit it on the floor.

"All right, Allison and Holland outside," he said.

"What the hell for?" Hugh said.

"There's a mule stuck in the mudbank a half-mile downriver. You're going to pull him out."

"Who says we got to do it?" Hugh said.

"Landry wants two men, and he didn't say nothing about taking a vote."

"Holland just come out of the dog box," Hugh said.

"And I just had to empty out the slop jars after they was drinking all night. Things is tough everywhere these days."

Hugh bit a chew off his tobacco twist, put the rest inside his jumper, and stood up from his bunk.

"Where'd you get that?" the trusty said.

"I took it away from a trusty that wanted to make my day a little harder."

"You give me what you got there and you can sleep this morning."

"You know why you're a trusty? It's because you like toting for them and cleaning their slop jars and jumping around like a monkey on a wire. They could turn you loose and you'd find somebody just like them. They understand your kind real good."

"You know what's going to happen to you, Allison? You're going to grow old in here. You're going to forget when you come in or how many years you spent here, and you'll start pissing on yourself at night and putting your food in your beard and asking people when they're going to let you out."

Hugh leaned toward the bars and spit a stream of tobacco juice into the rain.

"Maybe I ought to tell you something to make your day more interesting," he said. "A couple of them trusties you bunk with was

with me and Wiley Harpe and Sam Mason on the Natchez Trace.
They owe me a lot of favors, number one being I never told about
a whole family they tomahawked to death up in Tennessee. Now,
you think about that awhile, pigshit."

Hugh took the manacles out of the trusty's hands, snapped one
iron band around his wrist and the other on Son's, turned the key
on each lock, and handed it back to the trusty.

"Come on, Son, let's get that mule out of there so we can get
some rest today," he said.

They and the trusty went to the tool house for a block and
tackle, then they followed Alcide Landry on his dun horse down
the river bank to where the mule was stuck up to its flanks in the
soft mud by the water's edge. The rain clicked flatly on Landry's
gum coat, and when he twisted in the saddle to see that they
stayed in step behind him, Son saw the white, drawn emptiness
in his face and the resentful narrowed eyes which meant that his
older brother had probably forced him to go after the mule.

An oak tree dripping with Spanish moss hung out over the
mudbank where the mule was caught, and while the trusty climbed
along the limb with the block and tackle knotted around his waist,
Son and Hugh waded into the shallows and mud and began working
a double cinch under the mule's stomach. The water became so
clouded that they couldn't see their hands under the surface, and
each time they tried to tighten the cinch the mule drew in all its
breath until its sides were as hard as a barrel.

"I'll teach you about that trick, you piece of glue," Hugh said,
and drew back his huge fist and slammed it into the mule's rib
cage.

The mule's breath went out with a wheeze, and they slipped
the cinch tight and attached the iron rings to the block and tackle
that hung from the oak limb. Alcide Landry watched them silently
from atop his horse, back under the driest branches of the spreading
oak. Son thought his face looked even whiter than it had earlier.

They pulled the mule free from the mud and whipped it across
the scrotum with willow switches until it finally labored with its
hooves and knees out of the shallows onto the sand. The rain was
cold and driving hard now, and islands of dead trees floated past
them in the center of the river. The trusty climbed out on the oak

limb and tried to unknot the rope on the block and tackle, but the rain had swollen the hemp. He tore a fingernail and held his hand under his armpit.

"I can't untie the sonofabitch with the weight hanging on it," he said, his small body like a wooden clothespin on the limb. "Swing it back up behind me somewheres."

"I reckon things is tough everywhere these days," Hugh said.

"You better check on what's in your dinner bowl the next time you eat," the trusty said.

"Why don't you just stay up there and they'll bring their slop jars to you?"

"Let's get on with it and get out of here," Son said.

"*Vite.* Too much time," Landry said.

"He wants to get back to his whiskey pretty bad, don't he?" Hugh said softly. He took the heavy block and tackle and swung it as hard as he could toward the back of the tree. It knocked into the trunk and swung back over the water again.

"Too much time," Landry said, and rode his horse out from under the tree to the edge of the river. Water dripped off the brim of his hat, but his face was as white and dry as paper. Son could see the small cracks in his lips, and he remembered what his own face had looked like in a mirror after he had been drinking for two days in New Orleans.

Hugh swung the block again at the tree, his thick arms high over his head, and it looped up into the branches, disappearing for a moment in a shower of raindrops, then swung back into its trajectory and caught Alcide Landry with its full weight squarely in the face.

His boots hadn't been in the stirrups, and the blow knocked him backward off the rump of the horse into the water. His nose was roaring blood and there was a piece of tooth stuck on his lip. He sat in the shallows with his legs spread apart and his arms propped behind him while his stovepipe hat floated away from him. Son stared at him and felt his heart sink with a fear that he had never known before at the penal camp. He looked at Hugh, whose face was as blank as his own must have been, except for the black marble eye that had a frightful light in it.

"We're in a shitpot full of it now," Hugh said. "Let's finish it."

He ran through the shallows in his bare feet and came down into Landry's chest with his knees, then began swinging into his face with both fists.

"What are you doing?" the trusty shouted from the oak limb. "Do you know what his brother will do to us for this? I ain't a part of it. I ain't here."

"Get a stone, a stick, anything," Hugh said. "I can't hold him under."

Landry's head came up from the water, the blood and wet sand streaming from his face. His eyes were crossed and there was a deep gash like an indented star in the middle of his forehead.

"Damn it, Son, get something," Hugh said, then poised his fist in midair and got off Landry's chest and stumbled up onto the sand. He looked furiously for a weapon, picked up a rotted cypress knot and threw it aside; then he kicked at Landry's head once with his bare foot and fell backward in the sand. Landry got to his hands and knees, a clot of blood dripping off his tongue, his gum coat tangled around his body, and began crawling back to where his horse stood under the oak.

"Get the manacles. They're on his pommel," Hugh said.

The horse flipped his head at the collapsed reins when Son got close to him, and he was barely able to pull the looped chain from the pommel before the horse spooked back into the trees. Son ran back to the water's edge, where Hugh was trying to roll Landry over on his back.

"We can lock him and the trusty around the tree," Son said. "They won't come looking for them till this afternoon."

"Then do it. I can't keep holding him by myself. Grab his arm."

"He's slippery as bear grease."

"Then sit on him."

The three of them slipped and rolled in the wet sand, the manacles swinging in the air, then one of Landry's hands went inside his coat.

"Oh shit, Hugh. He's got a pistol in there."

"Hold his arm. Don't let him get it out." Hugh wrapped the chain once around the guard's throat and pulled it tight. Landry's head snapped backward as though he had been dropped from a gallows. His eyes bulged, his tongue came out, and his free hand pushed desperately at Hugh's face.

"Pull on the other end," Hugh said.

"Hugh—"

"Do it, you hear me."

"Just get the gun from him. We can't—"

"Son, he's cocked it. Lean into that chain."

Son saw the barrel's stiff outline pointed at his stomach. He kicked at Landry and turned his head away, his teeth clenched and his eyes closed, just as the ball tore through the coat in an explosion of dirty smoke and flattened into his rib cage.

He knew that it was still raining because he could see the water dimpling in the river, but there was no sound. The horizon tilted, and he saw the willows and oaks and cypresses green against the sky, and a riderless horse was bolting in a shower of sand down the river bank. He wiped his mouth quietly, swallowed, and tried to concentrate his vision on the horse that was now far down the river, the empty stirrups flying back against its flanks.

He felt Hugh tearing away the striped jumper from his side. Over Hugh's shoulder he could see the guard sitting upright in the sand, his face dead and staring like a gargoyle's.

"You ain't gut shot, are you?" Hugh said.

"I don't know."

"Spit in my hand."

"What?"

"Do what I say. Spit."

Son leaned over into Hugh's palm.

"Clear as spring water," Hugh said. "I knowed he couldn't get you."

"Did you—"

"I jerked back on the chain just when he let off at you. It don't take a lot to bust it sometimes."

Son pressed his hand against his side and felt the wetness run between his fingers.

"How bad is it?" he said.

"I reckon the ball's still in there, but it ain't deep. I'll get some cobweb back in them trees and catch up the mule and then we're going swimming."

The trusty climbed down from the oak and stood several feet from them. The rain clicked steadily on his straw hat.

"I can't go back there," he said.

"That's right, but you ain't going nowhere with us," Hugh said.

"I only had two years to go. You done all this."

"You don't think too good, do you?" Hugh said. "I just as soon kill you like I done him. You best go after that horse while you got the chance and head for Mississippi. But you remember one thing. If we run across you again, or if you give the law a sniff of where we're at, I'm going to finish you the way Wiley Harpe used to do it. I'll gut you like a fish, fill your insides with rocks, and sink you in the river."

The trusty looked at the insane light in Hugh's black marble eye and began walking down the river in the sharply etched tracks of the riderless horse.

"I don't know if I can swim it," Son said.

"There's a narrow place two miles down from here. We're going to hold onto that mule's tail and go right across it. Then we ain't stopping till we see Texas."

"Get the cobweb, Hugh, and let's get out of here."

The river narrowed just before it made a mile-wide bend with a steamboat landing on the far side. There were sandbars in the middle of the current with willow trees on them, and the bleached wreck of a flatboat lay on its side against the distant line of flooded cypress. Son tied the jumper tightly around his wound, unlaced his boots, and hung them around his neck.

"I don't know if I told you this," Hugh said, "but in Kentucky they don't teach you how to swim. If I slip off that mule's tail, don't come after me."

"You crazy old sonofabitch. This is a hell of a time to tell me that."

"Boy, we ain't got too many selections in the matter."

They whipped the mule into the water, then pushed at its rump until it stumbled off the shelf of mudbank into the current. Its eyes were wide with fright, its teeth bared and its nostrils dilated for air above the eddies swirling around its neck.

"Swim, you old shitpot, or you drown with us," Hugh said.

They held onto its tail with one hand and fought to keep their heads above the water with the other. Son's boots felt like iron weights hanging from his neck, and he thought he could feel the pistol ball grating against a rib each time he swung out his free arm. Up the river, he heard the whistle of a steamboat; then it came into view, low and massive and gleaming whitely in the rain.

"That's our luck, ain't it?" Hugh said. "They'll probably stop and try to pick us up."

The mule reached the first sandbar in the middle of the current, and kicked its way up out of the shallows as soon as they let go of its tail. They lay on the sand, their faces on their arms, their chests heaving. Son twisted the jumper tighter on his wound, and a spiderweb of pink ran down his side.

"Two hundred more yards," Hugh said. "Then we ain't got nothing to worry about except cottonmouths and mosquitoes."

"He's going to come after us. You know that, don't you?"

"He'll do that, all right. But it's a different game now. He don't have the edge no more."

They went into the water with the mule again, and as the dessicated wreck of the flatboat on the far bank came nearer, Son looked up the river at the huge paddle-wheeler approaching them, the smoke blowing off its scrolled stacks, the latticework on the upper deck splashing with rain, and he wondered at all the wealth inside, the grand salons where fortunes in cotton were won and lost with a casual throw of a playing card.

"Forget about it. The likes of us ain't ever going to ride in something like that," Hugh said.

When the mule's hooves hit bottom and its shoulders suddenly rose from the water's surface, Son felt something tear loose inside him like a black marble rolling into a socket of pain. The mule's tail slipped out of his hand, and the soft brown current moved over his head and filled his ears with a quiet hum. He opened his eyes once and saw that life was simply an infinite green expanse of light that he could breathe as easily as a fish.

Hugh's rough hand broke the water and pulled his head up by the hair.

"We done made it, Son," he said. "What's the matter with you? We ain't going to see Jesus for a long time yet."

CHAPTER
TWO

By the next morning his side was aflame, and a black fluid leaked from his jumper and ran down into his dirty breeches. He held onto Hugh's waist to keep from falling off the mule's rump, and when he closed his eyes he heard the rain ticking in the trees overhead.

They were deep into a green woods, and the mist hung in pools around the trunks of the oaks. Last night they had ridden for several hours on a road under a smoky moon, but at the first gray light on the horizon they had moved back into the woods again, and now they were not sure where they were. In fact, in the dark they couldn't be sure that they had continued riding westward.

Late that afternoon Son heard the cicadas begin humming in the trees. He looked upward and saw the limbs sweep over him, then felt his body topple backward off the mule's rump. He landed in the wet leaves with his arms spread out by his sides. Hugh knelt over him and bit a chew off his tobacco.

"You just can't make it like this, can you?" he said. "Look, it opens up down yonder, and we can't go no farther in these convict clothes. We passed an empty nigger cabin back there, and I'm going to have to leave you there while I go get us a few things."

"Maybe you better take off, Hugh. They're behind us someplace."

"They're a long way behind us. If I figure right, we're about halfway to Opelousas, and after that the Sabine is just down the pike. Get your foot in my hand and set your butt up on that mule."

That night Hugh left him in the cabin and rode back toward the edge of the woods. Son slept on the dirt floor under the portion of cabin roof that hadn't caved in, and in his feverish dreams he saw a gargoyle face screaming without sound from a twisted chain.

It had stopped raining and the false dawn showed through the cabin window when he heard horses in the leaves outside. He sat upright, his hand on his side and his heart beating, and stared hard at the frame of gray light through the cabin door.

"Boy, you either bled yourself white or I scared religion into you," Hugh said. He held a cloth sack in his hand, and behind him Son saw two horses tethered to the root of an oak tree.

"Where you been?"

"At a settlement about five miles south. I got everything we need, including two horses from Andy Jackson's soldier boys."

"You stole horses from the army?"

"You damn right I did. I took a redcoat ball in my leg at Chalmette in 1815 for him and I reckon he owes me that much. Them soldier boys was drunk in the tavern, and I walked their horses right down the road while they was rolling dice for drinks."

"I can't ride no more, Hugh."

"Yes, you can, because I'm going to whittle that ball right out of your side. Look what I got in the bag. There was two stores down the pike from the tavern, and I got into the back of both of them." He loosened the drawstring on the bag and took out a huge knife with a bone handle and a whetstone in the buckskin scabbard, three slabs of cured bacon, a wax-sealed jar of honeycombs, a jar of molasses, two shirts and pairs of trousers, two straw hats and a bottle of clear whiskey. "But look what I found under the counter. It's an old one, but you can put the ball in a pig's snout at twenty yards with it."

He held an English flintlock pistol and a brass powder flask and three molded bullets in both hands.

"The flint is pretty wore down, but I'll still take it over a wet cap when you got to count on it," he said.

"The high sheriff is going to be all over these woods, Hugh."

"No, he ain't. I put them locks back on the doors just like they was when I went in. When they notice something's gone, they won't have no idea of when it was stole. But right now you got to do some drinking. In fact, you're going to get drunker than a bluejay in a mulberry tree." Hugh uncorked the bottle of whiskey and took a drink from the neck. He swished it in his mouth and spit it on the dirt floor of the cabin.

"I feel sorry for you," he said. "I'd rather have that ball in my side than drink this. They must have put lye in the mash."

He handed the bottle to Son and began honing the knife on the whetstone. The knife was made from a wagon spring, and had been heated in a smithy's forge and shaped and hammered on an anvil until it was as smooth and thin as a metal dollar and had the fragile edge of a razor.

Son's empty stomach tightened with each swallow from the bottle and the corn taste of the whiskey welled up into his throat and nose and made tears run from his eyes. He thought he was going to vomit, and he set the bottle upright beside him, but Hugh picked it up and pushed it against his mouth again.

"Let it boil down inside you," he said. "A couple more swallows and it won't fight back no more. In the meantime, I'm going to tell you how Micajah Harpe had his head cut off."

The whiskey ran over Son's mouth, and the back of his throat felt as though he had swallowed a tack.

"You're a crazy bastard, Hugh. You busted your head open too many times in the dog box."

Hugh untied the jumper from Son's waist and peeled the bloody cloth back from the wound. Then he wiped the metal filings off the knife's edge on his breeches and poured whiskey on both sides of the blade.

"Put this tobacco back in your teeth and don't swallow it," he said. "The ball's worked up on your rib, and I'm going to cut an X on it and pop it right out of there. It's going to hurt like somebody put an iron on you, but as soon as it's out you'll feel all that fire drain out of you."

"Get to it."

"Now, let me tell you about Micajah," Hugh said, and pressed the knife's edge along the swollen lump in Son's rib cage. "Him and Wiley was about the meanest sonsofbitches I ever knowed. They didn't care no more about killing a man than stepping on a frog. Sometimes I tell people about how I was with the gang when somebody's giving me a bad time, mainly because it scares the hell out of them, but to tell you the truth I'm ashamed of some of the things I know about. That wasn't no made-up story about filling up people's insides with rocks and throwing them in the river."

He slipped the knife deeper, and the inflamed skin peeled back from the flattened lead ball. Son's eyes were red, and tobacco juice slid from the side of his mouth.

"But Micajah finally got his," Hugh said. "After he killed some people the high sheriff and some others run him to ground and put a ball in his spine. He was flopping around in the dirt like a fish that was throwed up on the bank. Then this one fellow put a knife in his throat and run it around his neck just like you core an apple.

Son clenched his hand over his eyes and tried to spit the tobacco from his mouth. His heart was thundering in his chest.

"Micajah looked up at this fellow and said, 'You're a damn rough butcher but cut and be done.' When they got his head off they stuck it on a pole in the road, and I reckon his grinning skull is still staring out at people today.

"I done got it, Son. Landry must have melted down a half-bar to make that ball. It's a wonder he didn't tear the ribs plumb out of your side."

Son choked on the threads of tobacco in his throat and tried to wave at Hugh, then he heard the rain ticking in the leaves again and felt the smoky green morning light fill the inside of the cabin.

Five days later they stood on a red clay bluff above the Sabine River with low rolling hills of pine trees on the far side. Hawks floated high on the windstream in the clear sky, and the sunlight was so brilliant on the countryside that it hurt Son's eyes. Below the bluff was a shack where a ferry-keeper lived, and the ferry itself was pulled up into the shallows and swinging slowly in the current from the pulley rope.

"How bad you leaking?" Hugh said.

"It's holding."

"You want to eat what we got left of the bacon before we cross?"

"Save it. I got a notion we ain't going to find nothing more to eat for a while," Son said.

"We'll get something off this fellow down here."

"Hugh, I don't want us to steal no more."

"I ain't going to steal nothing. You think I want to leave a trail of robberies all the way across Louisiana and Texas for Emile Landry to follow? I'm just going to swap this fellow something for a little food. I shouldn't have let you talk me into burying them saddles. We could probably get a whole sack of supplies for them."

"That's smart, ain't it? Trading off stolen army saddles. Why don't we leave our names while we're at it?"

"All right. Let's go find out if Texas has changed any since I was there last."

Son held his hand tight to his side while they rode down the bluff. Hugh kicked at the shack door with his boot without dismounting from his horse.

"Hey, in there, we need a ride across," he said.

A filthy, unshaven man in buckskin clothes stepped out into the sunlight. His skin was sallow and his eyes a stagnant green. Son couldn't tell if the fetid odor he smelled came from the man or inside the cabin.

"Damn, what you got in that shack, mister?" Hugh said.

"I got a Choctaw woman cooking tripe. It's twenty-five cents a bowl if you want some."

"You keep it," Hugh said. "We just need a ride and some bacon or jerky if you got it."

"I don't run no grocery store, and the trip across is a dollar a man. I don't take scrip, either."

"A dollar. Eating them pig guts has hurt your brain," Hugh said.

"You can swim it, then," the man said. "But them horses won't find no ford. Even the Indians don't cross it when it's this high."

"We ain't got two dollars, mister," Son said.

"I tell you what. I'll take that rusty pistol and the powder flask."

"I might give you something else out of this pistol," Hugh said.

"No, you ain't. Both of them horses has U.S. brands on them, and you're running for your ass right now."

"Give him the pistol and the flask," Son said.

"He's a squaw-man robber."

"Give them to him."

Hugh's black, deformed eye stared hotly at the ferry-keeper, then he took the flintlock from his trousers and slipped the leather cord of the powder flask off his shoulder.

"You got something else to eat in there besides tripe?" Son said. "We don't need much. Maybe some fatback."

"You bought yourself the float across and that's all. Ride your horses down the plank and tie them on the back end. I can't get off the mudbank with the weight up front."

They walked their horses onto the ferry, the hooves clopping on the planed cypress boards, and tethered them to the back rail. Son slid off his horse and had to support himself momentarily against the horse's neck. The ferry moved out into the current, straining against the pulley rope that stretched from one bank to the other. Sweat boiled off the ferry-keeper's face as he pulled on the rope with his wasted arms; then he walked the length of the boat with a long pole stuck into the river bottom. On the Texas side of the river the swollen carcass of a drowned fawn lay in the shadows, and Son could see the sharp backs of enormous garfish that were tearing at its flanks.

The ferry came to rest in a small inlet surrounded with willow trees, and the ferry-keeper dropped his pole on the deck.

"Boy, you look like a dog's been chewing on your side," he said.

"Listen, you asshole," Hugh said. "You say anything more and I'm going to slice your ears off. And if you tell anybody we been through here and I hear about it, I'll be back and burn your shack down with you and your squaw in it."

"I get them every day like you two," the ferry-keeper said. "All of you are running for Texas to hide in Sam Houston's army. You don't bother me none."

"Is that a fact?" Hugh said, and rode his horse at the man and knocked him against the wood railing.

The ferry-keeper stumbled backward, his eyes wide with surprise. "What are you doing?" he said.

Hugh hit him again with the horse and knocked him backward another five feet.

"Just keep on walking," he said, then herded the man as he would a calf off the back end of the ferry. "That's right, splash around in it a bit. You can sure use it. In fact, you smell like somebody painted shit on you."

They rode their horses up the clay bank into a stand of pine trees. The brown needles were thick on the ground and smelled sweet in the wind blowing through the trunks.

"I should have got our pistol and flask back before I run his ass off the boat," Hugh said.

"Then he could tell the law we stole from him."

"He ain't going to tell the law nothing. He didn't breathe real good there for a minute when I told him I'd make stubs out of his ears. I should have told him I knowed James Bowie. A turd would have rolled out of his pants leg for sure.

"You knew Bowie?"

"I used to play cards with him in New Orleans. Then I run into him a couple of times when I shot buffalo for the Mexicans in Texas."

"Hugh, have you really done all this stuff?"

"You make up your own mind about it. But I drank many a bottle of whiskey with him and rode alligators with him, too. Jim was always ready for fun or a prank. One night I played cards with him and Jean Lafitte on Royal Street until seven o'clock in the morning. Jim ordered us brandy and coffee and cigars and then we walked down to a pit by the river that had an alligator in it as thick across as your horse. He got the darkies to haul it out of the pit and then he rode it plumb down to the market and fed it a meat pie in the cafe. But he wasn't nobody to fool with, either. I heared different stories about him and that knife of his—that him and another fellow fought a duel with their wrists tied together, that another time they nailed their buckskin pants legs to a log and went at it—but I know for a fact he got into it on a sandbar out from Natchez and he cut a fellow up after they already put two pistol balls in him."

"I never asked you this, but why'd you kill that fellow in New Orleans?"

"Every night in the pen when I heered the boys in the dog boxes and thought about all the time I had ahead of me, I tried to figure out that same question myself. We was playing *bouree* down by the nigger quarters and I seen him reach under his leg for a card. I told him all that money on the table was mine, and he came up with a dirk in his hand. So I picked up a full bottle and busted his head apart like a flower pot.

"But lookie here, let's talk about where we're going and what our selections are."

The trees had become more evenly spaced, and Son could see the rolling green country of east Texas ahead of him.

"How the hell should I know?" Son said. "I never been in Texas. I don't know what's out there."

"A few thousand Mexican soldiers that's been shot at by Americans."

"Hugh, you can really lead us someplace, can't you?"

"Like I said before, when you break out of prison you don't draw the best card hand in the world."

"What do you want to do?"

"There ain't nothing but Indians north of us, and the closest town west is a good ways over on the Brazos. If we go south to the Gulf, maybe we can get a boat out of the whole damn country."

"To where?"

"Hell, I don't know everything. Any place where the law ain't coming up our ass."

"I ain't fond of leaving the country," Son said.

"What do you think you just left? This ain't the United States no more. All this belongs to Mexico. And right now them Mexicans hates the smell of anything white. I reckon sooner or later they're going to burn that ferry back there to keep the rest of us out."

"I don't want to ride no boat out of the country, Hugh. Let's go on up north through the Indians till we hit Arkansas."

"Some of Landry's piss must have been on that ball, because you got a fever in your brain. There's Comanches up there, and what they do to you when they catch you ain't something you want to study on. When I was hunting buffalo they caught one of my partners and roasted him over a fire. Before he was dead they cut off his arms and legs and left him in the coals. I didn't hunt buffalo no more after that, and I sure ain't going up in their country again.

"I don't even know why I'm talking to you like this. We're going south for the Gulf and we'll decide about the boat when we get there. We got almost nothing to eat, no gun, and your face is white as bird shit."

Two hours later they were following a deer trail along the bottom of a hill through a long stretch of piney woods when Hugh sawed in on the bit and grabbed Son's arm.

"You smell it?" he said.

"What?"

"An Indian camp."

"I don't smell nothing."

"They're smoking jerky. You hear the dog?"

At first, Son could only hear the hum of his fever in his ears, then when the wind dropped below the trees he heard the angry bark of a dog violating the air.

"They tie a mean one up outside of camp so nobody don't sneak up on them," Hugh said. "They're probably Choctaws, and that means we probably get something to eat tonight and a place to sleep besides the woods."

"They're savages."

"Listen, there ain't nothing more savage than a white man. I didn't tell you the rest of that story about my partner getting roasted. The others with us went back to that village at night and killed everybody in it. They even scalped the children."

In his mind, Son again saw the bodies of his parents in the lot by the burned cabin. His father's scorched eyes were staring like pieces of fish scale, and his severed fingers had been stuck in his mouth.

The pine trees began to thin and they followed a clear stream with a silt bottom to the edge of a clearing. A dozen tepees, made of stitched deerskins and shaved pines, were arranged in a circle back toward the trees. In the center of the clearing, strips of venison hung from racks over wet fires, and Indian women were throwing handfuls of pine needles into the smoke. Son saw thirty to forty horses penned back in the woods on the far side of the camp.

"That's too many horses for this bunch," Hugh said. "I got a notion we're about to take up company with thieves."

They walked their horses into the clearing, and Son felt the wound in his side begin to throb. The Indian women looked at them like statues in the smoke.

"I sure wish I had a drink of that bad whiskey right now," Hugh said.

"I thought you said they was Choctaws, that they wasn't savages."

"You can't always tell if your selections are correct."

"The next time I break out of jail, I ain't going with a crazy man."

"Be quiet, and don't show them you're scared. An Indian can't tolerate two things, and that's fear and lying."

"Look at that one in the armor. Where did he get that at?"

They watched a tall Indian in a coat of Spanish mail and a pair of buckskin breeches walk toward them from a tepee that was covered with blue and yellow designs. The mail he wore overlapped like bird's feathers, and the area around his bare arms was eaten with rust.

"You better think of something good to say. He don't look like he wants us here," Son said.

"He wants something, all right. He seen them Uncle Sam brands, and he wants to add them to his collection."

The Indian looked up at them with his opaque face and hazel eyes, then put his thumb into the mouth of Son's horse and pushed back its lips over the teeth. There was a hard line of callous across his chest where the top of his armor rubbed against the skin.

"We want to trade," Hugh said. .

"Where got?" the Indian said.

"We bought them off the army in Louisiana," Hugh said.

"Soldiers no sell horses. Where got?"

"We got them the same place you bought all them quarter horses with mixed brands back in the trees."

"Take it easy, Hugh," Son said, quietly.

"We'll give you one horse for food and a gun with powder and shot."

The Indian looked again at the horse's teeth, then into the corners of its eyes.

"Sit in my tepee. We smoke there," he said.

"We ain't here to bargain. We want food and a gun," Son said.

"Wait out here," Hugh said.

"While you swap off my horse?"

"Only old man come," the Indian said.

Son watched Hugh and the Indian walk back to the tepee and sit inside the open flap, then he looked at the women who were still staring at him out of the smoke. Their thighs were wide and thick from childbearing, their shoulders rounded from years of stooping to pick up firewood and wash clothes in a stream, and the only thing feminine about them were the fish combs they wore in the tight buns on the backs of their head. Their faces were absolutely without expression, as though they had been snipped out of dried buffalo hide.

Son watched the grease glisten on the venison and drip hissing into the fire, and the smell made his empty stomach ache. The sun was hot on his head, a clear line of sweat ran out of his hair, and his side began to stiffen and throb worse from sitting in one position. He became angrier at Hugh's delay in the tent and the fact that they had stopped in the village at all. The Indian was smoking the pipe and speaking in his own language and raising the bowl toward the four corners of the earth. Back in Tennessee mountain people called them red niggers, because in the Cumberlands slaves had little value and Indians even less. And that's what they are, Son thought. Not worth a darky's sweat.

Hugh stepped out of the tent and squinted his walleye at the hard blue sky. The Indian still sat inside in his rusted coat of mail.

"What did that thief give you for my horse?" Son said.

"It ain't exactly just your horse."

"So tell me what we traded off. I'm surprised you still got your britches on."

"Well, we kind of took the best of our choices in the situation. I'm letting him have both horses. We can't go riding across Texas with stolen brands on them, nohow. Besides, mine's got a splayed hoof that ole Iron Jacket don't know about yet."

"What the hell are we supposed to ride out of here?" Son said.

"That's it. We ain't going nowhere for a while. He give us one of his tepees, all the food we want, and we can stay till we get a mind to move on. Lookie, you must have leaked a boot-full of blood since I cut that ball out of you, and if we keep riding you're going to fall off your horse and be dead before you hit the earth. You know why he didn't want you in his tepee? He seen your side, and he said you was just about ready for a hole in the ground."

"So we give up both of our horses for some food and a tent."

"There was something extra in the deal. He threw in a Tonkawa woman to cook and tote for us."

"I should have figured it. You got more rut in you than brains, Hugh."

"I done the best I could, boy. He didn't have no guns to trade because the Mexicans took them all away from him. We can't make the Gulf or the Brazos with you squirting like a broke pipe every time we climb a hill, and he was set on taking both horses and giving us the woman or making no deal at all. Now, that's just where it stands. If you want, we'll keep on a-going. But you remember Emile Landry is back there somewhere, and we ain't going to be worth horse piss on a rock if he runs up on us the way we are now."

"All right. But after I mend, where we going to get horses?"

"I come up with these two, didn't I? Besides, Iron Jacket says the Mexicans got an army post about ten miles north of here, and stealing from them bastards is patriotic."

Son slid off his horse in front of their tepee and limped inside. The dirt floor was covered with buffalo robes and dirty horse blankets, and there was a fire pit in the center circled with blackened rocks. The stitched buckskin hides at the bottom of the tepee had been rolled up a foot from the ground to create a circular draft inside, and the chimney at top where the poles were bound together with braided hide was opened against the sky.

"Take your shirt off and give me them bloody rags and I'll let them wash out in the stream," Hugh said. "I'll get that Tonkawa woman to cook us a whole shitpot of venison stew. I ain't been so hungry since I got froze in for five days up on the plains."

"Don't them Tonkawas live up by the Comanches?"

"That's right, but they ain't like the Comanches. In fact, all the Comanches ain't bad, either. Their women is right nice-looking. They're tall with long legs and they got skin the color of a penny. Just like that one out there. I seen her when we first rode into camp. She didn't look nothing like them squat little frogs throwing pine needles in the fire. Iron Jacket said she must have been a hand-blower when she was with the Tonkawas, because they sold her to some Mexican buffalo hunters, and after they come back to the Sabine with their skins they traded her to him for two horses."

"What's a hand-blower?"

"That's an Indian woman that sneaks off from the camp at night and blows in her palms like an owl till her buck finds her. But she makes him run all over the place first. She'll hide in the brush and hoot, and just when he thinks he's going to start courting she'll take off again. It ain't much different from what some of our women do, but Indians run them out of camp."

Son lay his head back on a horse blanket and looked up at the blue circle of sky through the top of the tepee. There was a burned strip of cloud on the edge of the sun, and he smelled the horse sweat in the blanket under his head and felt the coarse hair of the buffalo robe against his bare shin; then Hugh's thick body backed out in silhouette through the tepee's open flap and he felt himself pulled away into a dream of green mountains covered with poplars, birches, and white oaks, with smoke drifting from the limestone chimneys of the cabins down in the hollow.

He smelled venison when he awoke toward evening. It was cool and Hugh was poking sticks into the fire in the center of the tepee. The draft through the open flap swirled the smoke in a circle up through the chimney. The Tonkawa woman sat on her knees against the back of the tepee.

"This is White-Man's-Woman," Hugh said. "At least that's the name these Choctaws give her. She won't tell me her real name."

She was tall, with straight hair over her shoulders, and the deerskin dress she wore was blackened by the smoke from cook fires. Son thought he could smell the faint odor of dried animal grease in her direction, like the odor of a coon skin that had been fleshed out and left to cure in the sun.

"Give him one of them bowls," Hugh said. "He ain't had no venison since them Frenchies stuck him in jail."

The woman removed a clay bowl of stew from a flat rock next to the fire and handed it to Son. As she leaned forward out of the gloom into the firelight, he saw the black, hard expression in her eyes.

"You sure you want this in our tent tonight?" he said to Hugh.

"You don't know nothing about Indians. We'll treat her a lot better than Iron Jacket and them fat squaws of his, and she knows it. There ain't nothing worse than being a woman prisoner of other squaws. Besides, like I told you, she belonged to a couple of Mexican skin hunters before she got here, and them bastards ain't hardly human."

"I'd sleep on my knife tonight, anyway."

"I'm planning to sleep on something else."

"You can't stay out of trouble, can you?" Son said, and drank the stew broth from the edge of the bowl. It scalded his lips and made his eyes water, but the taste was so good that he couldn't take his mouth away.

Son picked the meat out of the bowl with his fingers and sucked the fine bones clean. He leaned toward the fire to fill the bowl again, but the woman took it from his hand and dipped it into the small black pot for him. She had a white scar, like a piece of string, that extended from the corner of one eye.

"Some of this don't taste like deer to me," he said.

"They put some dog in it. Indians think that's eating high up on the back quarter."

"I want to get out of here, Hugh. I don't care where we go."

"You're stubborn, ain't you? There's no talking to you about anything."

"We'll get horses off them Mexicans, and we'll take our chances out there." He waved his arm in a vague way toward the western side of the tepee.

"We'll go when we're ready, and you ain't ready. I don't have no intention of going to prison, and I ain't stopping a ball because you can't keep up."

"I ain't held you back since you whittled on my side, have I?"

"You didn't do nothing to make it easier, either."

"I didn't get asked to be taken along. You made damn sure back there in Louisiana that we'll probably run till they bounce us off a tree."

"You rather be back in the dog box or listening to a quirt sing down on your butt?"

They were both silent a moment in their anger, and a gust of wind through the flap blew a shower of sparks up toward the chimney. The woman looked at them cautiously from where she sat on her knees.

"The fall's coming on, aint it?" Hugh said. "These tepees ain't worth wet paper when it starts to get cold. I don't know how all these dumb bastards get through a winter."

"If you want to cut it up between us and catch that boat on the Gulf, go ahead on your own, Hugh. I ain't going to put a stick between your legs."

"Who's going to keep you from falling off your horse again?

Tomorrow we're going to find out just where we're at and see what our selections are. I ain't too fond of this savage living myself. I had too much of it up there on the plains with the Comanches and Tonkawas."

"This afternoon you said they was all right."

"You can't always tell what you'll say in the afternoon. What I had in mind for us is more like going on to Bexar and meeting up with Jim Bowie. A man in jail told me that he married into Santa Anna's family and he's got more money and land now than an English lord."

"No magic water tonight," the woman said.

"What?" Son said.

"Don't pay no attention," Hugh said.

"The magic water is bad," she said.

"Indians think when white people are mad at each other they been drinking whiskey," Hugh said. "They drink this busthead stuff full of snakes' heads and tobacco spit that the traders give them, and it drives them crazy. Later, they can't explain what they done, and they call it the magic water."

He turned to the woman.

"We ain't got no whiskey," he said. "I wouldn't bring none into an Indian camp, nohow."

"She must be scared of it, all right," Son said.

"Them Mexicans that owned her probably got drunk sometimes and beat up on her. I knowed a skin hunter once that made his squaw walk barefoot all day because she burned his breakfast."

Hugh looked again at the woman.

"We ain't like that," he said. "I'd never hit on a woman and I don't get drunk."

"You ain't had a chance to in three years."

"It don't matter. The whiskey ain't been made that can get me drunk. And I never hit a woman in my life."

"You sure court in a strange way, Hugh."

"I don't know why I took you along. You don't know a thing, do you?"

"Sleep on your knife tonight."

"That's what I mean. You're too young to know the difference between a slop jar and a bowl of grits, but you always got something to say to an older man."

The last of the twilight began to fade in the trees outside, and Son could hear the starlings and whippoorwills circling their nests. A steady wind was blowing out of the pines against the side of the tepee. The fire burned down in the circle of stones, and the ashes rose and fell in the puffs of cool air through the flap.

"Where you sleeping tonight?" Hugh said.

"Not out there, if that's what you got in mind. I ain't going to wake up with them savages eating on me."

"All right. I ain't embarrassed by what's natural. Just make yourself a pallet over there in the corner."

That night the moon was full and directly overhead in the clear sky like a hard piece of ivory. Son heard movement a few feet from him, and he looked up to see Hugh trying to pull off his trousers from a sitting position. He worked them down over his knees, his ruined face concentrated with effort in the moonlight through the chimney, then fell backward in his blankets when he pulled them from his ankles. He crawled on his hands and knees toward the woman, and then there was the wheezing rush of breath like a bull's when he fell with his full weight on top of her.

In one motion she twisted out from under him and grabbed a two-foot piece of unburned pine wood from the edge of the fire pit and swung it across the bridge of his nose. He reared upward on his knees with one hand welded against his face and the other trying to push her backward into the buffalo skins. She swung again, this time across his temple, and Son heard the wood knock into bone. Hugh's walleye protruded even farther from the socket, and his mouth fell open as though his jaws had been broken. There was a spiderweb of blood around his nose.

"Don't hit him no more," Son said.

She raised the wood again, but Son caught it behind her shoulder and pulled it from her palm. Her hot eyes looked wildly into his face.

"He shouldn't have bothered you like that, but he's too old to take them kind of licks."

He could see the pulse jumping in her neck, and he smelled again the dried animal fat in her dress and hair.

"He's too old. Do you understand that? Only an old man would try to do something like that. He was in prison, and he ain't been around women in three years."

"What for?" she said.

"He was in trouble with a fellow in New Orleans."

"You ain't got to talk for me. Don't tell that crazy woman nothing," Hugh said. He sat on his bare buttocks amid the tangle of horse blankets and buffalo robes with his fingers pressed against the swelling knot on his temple. "I ought to knowed better than to try and top a Tonkawa hand-blower. Go on and get outside where you belong. You can stay with them fat frogs of Iron Jacket's."

"You started all this shit, Hugh."

"She can go back to jerking venison around that hot fire or lying with Mexicans. She ain't sleeping in here."

"You got your brains shook loose, or you're being a genuine sonofabitch."

"Tell her to get or you can go with her."

The woman walked outside into the moonlit center of the village and sat by the dead fire where the Choctaws had been smoking jerky that afternoon. Son stared through the flap at her immobile back and rigid head. He picked up a blanket and a buffalo robe and got to his feet.

"What are you doing?" Hugh said.

"Nothing."

He walked to where the woman sat and put the robe and blanket beside her. She glanced up at him, almost apprehensively, then fixed her eyes on the far side of the clearing. The skin on her face was tight from the cold.

"He ain't a bad man. He's just dumb sometimes," Son said.

She made no reply or even showed recognition that he was speaking to her.

"Look. Put them on. It's going to get a lot colder before the sun comes up."

The wind blew a long white crease in her hair.

"Suit yourself, but let me tell you something. Tomorrow he's going to feel bad about what he done, and he'll ask you to come back in and he won't bother you no more."

"He's like the Mexicans that killed Buffalo Hump. They take the women and use the men on the soldiers' town." She spoke across the dead ashes of the fire pit without looking up.

"He ain't like no Mexican. Who's this Buffalo Hump?"

"They took him away to work on the soldiers' town. When he ran away from them, they came back and killed him. Out there. In the trees."

"Hugh ain't like that. He hates them kind of people worse than you all do."

"They said Buffalo Hump stole one of the metal bottles with the magic water."

"I reckon there's something wrong with the words I use, because you ain't listening."

He left her there and went back inside the tepee and tied the flap on the lodge pole behind him. His bare chest and shoulders were tingling when he wrapped himself in a blanket next to the warm stones by the fire pit.

Hugh squinted at him with his bad eye.

"Did you learn anything out there?" he said.

"Yes, I did. Crazy people come in all colors. Or maybe some of them is just dumb and old. You study on that one."

"What?"

The next morning, when the sun rose yellow and cold through the pine trees and cast the first shadows through the red clay clearing, she still sat immobile by the edge of the fire pit, the buffalo robe draped in a hump over her head. Son's side was stiff when he awoke, and he lay in his blankets while Hugh coughed and hawked in his throat and tried to blow the dead fire into embers with his breath.

"Where in the hell are my britches?" Hugh said.

"The last time I seen them you couldn't throw them away fast enough."

Hugh hawked again and spit a wad of phlegm out the tepee flap.

"Where's that woman at? She should have had a breakfast fire going before we woke up."

"I think she's about *there*," Son said, and pointed his finger over his head without looking.

"Tell her to get her ass in here and go to work."

"I reckon I'll lay here awhile. My side's giving me a fit this morning."

"You think you're smart, don't you?"

"No, I just ain't learned to deal with these savages yet."

"There's a lot you ain't learned to deal with. That's for damn sure."

Hugh buttoned his trousers over his flat, knife-scarred stomach and pushed the tangle of gray-black hair out of his eyes.

"It ain't hard," Son said. "Just tell her you won't lose your britches again at night."

He watched Hugh walk barefoot across the clearing toward the woman, his brown triangular back knotted with effort as though he were walking on sharp stones. Son drank the last of the cold venison stew from the bowl the woman had set on a flat rock next to the fire the night before, and touched the hardening pucker of tissue around Hugh's knife marks in his rib cage. The blood had coagulated into the beginnings of a thick scab; he hadn't bled during the night, and the red swelling across the rib where the ball had struck him was now only a soft pink. When Hugh came back into the tepee with White-Man's-Woman and a bowl smoking with skinned catfish, he knew that everything was going to be all right for a while and Emile Landry and the law were lost somewhere behind them in the piney woods of east Texas.

Five days later, on a hard blue-gold afternoon, a contingent of Mexican cavalry rode their horses into the village.

CHAPTER

THREE

"Look at them arrogant characters," Hugh said. He and Son and White-Man's-Woman were outside the tepee, cleaning two raccoons that Hugh had knocked out of a tree with a club. "If that ain't a bunch of peacocks for you. They got enough braid and whistles on them to sink a horse through the ground."

They watched the formation of horses and uniformed Mexicans approach Iron Jacket's tepee, their silver scabbards and white bandoleers flashing in the sunlight. Iron Jacket stepped outside in his coat of mail with one coup feather in his hair. He looked absurd in front of the Mexican lieutenant.

"I think he's about to make a yellow puddle around his moccasins," Hugh said.

"They come for the horses at the last of the moon," the woman said.

"You mean they make that old horse thief steal for them?" Hugh said.

"He only steals from the Americans, and they take away half."

"That lieutenant must have his own business going then, because the Mexicans usually don't bother the Indians," Hugh said.

"You ever have trouble with them?" Son said.

"I had a bunch of them chase me across the Guadalupe once. But they ain't too bright in dealing with a white man. They tried to swim their horses after me, and they almost drowned with all that junk they wear on themselves."

"There go his horses. And I reckon ours, too," Son said.

They watched five enlisted men walk back into the pines and drop the shaved poles that formed one side of the horse pen. In fifteen minutes they had formed all the horses into two long strings, and they cantered them in a broken line back to the center of the clearing. Iron Jacket was talking rapidly to the lieutenant, his coup feather glued flat to the side of his face.

"I thought they only took half," Son said.

"At the last moon Iron Jacket had only nine horses," the woman said. "The Mexicans were mad, and they took away Buffalo Hump and his sons."

"I think that lieutenant just seen our brands," Hugh said.

The lieutenant walked to the two army horses and ran his hand over the thick, hairless scar in the flank of Son's roan.

"Why's he so interested in where they come from?" Son said.

"He don't want no trouble with any of Andy Jackson's soldier boys. He knows there's a whole army of them on the other side of the Sabine just waiting to come in and eat Texas up."

"I got another feeling, Hugh. He's heered something about us."

"Them Mexicans don't know nothing except what time to squat over the honey hole."

The lieutenant walked back to Iron Jacket and spoke briefly, then the Indian pointed in the direction of their tepee.

"He ain't exactly loyal about the people that live in his village, is he?" Son said.

"His balls are hanging over a fire right now, boy."

The Mexican officer motioned them toward him with a casual gesture of his fingers, as though he were dealing with a situation that was momentarily irritating and would soon be corrected. When they didn't move, his eyes became more concentrated, and fixed on them under the black bill of his cap.

"*Aqui,*" he said.

"How do you like a fellow like that telling you to fetch for him?" Son said.

"What language do you speak?" the Mexican said. "English? French? Come here."

Hugh wiped the raccoon blood off his knife blade and stuck it down in his trousers with the edge turned upward.

"Let him walk over here," Son said.

"He's got the guns and the men. We ain't got nothing but this pig sticker between us. Try to use your head awhile."

They walked across the clearing, and Son looked with more curiosity than heat into the officer's face. It didn't have the toughness of a soldier's, not the ones whom he had occasionally seen back in Tennessee or the mountain men who had fought with Andrew Jackson at Chalmette outside of New Orleans. Instead, the lines and the skin were soft, without windburn or scars or even a faint discoloration from the flint exploding into the flashpan of a rifle. The eyes went back to Europe, to an autocratic view of the world that he resented without even being able to understand it completely.

"Where did you get them?" the officer said.

"We got out of the army a couple of months ago and decided to try our luck over in Texas," Hugh said.

"How did you get the horses?"

"When him and me got discharged in Opelousas, we seen our mounts getting auctioned off to some Frenchies, and we bought them for five dollars apiece. Then we swapped them to Iron Jacket for a stay here and that squaw over by the tepee."

"The Americans don't sell their horses unless they burn the brand first."

"Yes, sir, that's true. But the first sergeant that was doing this sale is drunk most of the time, and he don't go about particulars when you show him a gold piece. Also, I was hurrying a little bit to get across the Sabine. I used to visit this lady that lives in St. Martinville—"

"What did you do with the saddles? Did you bury them along the road with the men you killed?"

"I don't think you're listening, Lieutenant. We didn't steal no horses, and we sure didn't kill nobody," Hugh said.

"How did you get those scars on your ankles?"

"I done some time when I was a kid."

"What do you care where them horses come from?" Son said. "You're taking them from the Indians, ain't you?"

"Son," Hugh said.

"Them horses is ours. We rode them over from Louisiana, and what we done over there ain't any business of yours."

"I think both of you are escaped convicts," the officer said.

The wind blew out of the pines and scattered ashes from the fire burning under the racks of venison in the center of the village. Son felt the wound in his side begin to quiver again.

"I done told you, Lieutenant," Hugh said. "I got these manacle scars when I was a boy over in Mississippi. All we want is to get up to the plains and make some money knocking down buffalo."

The lieutenant looked Son hard in the eyes.

"Do you know a Frenchman, a prison warden, named Landry?" he said.

Son stared back at him and forced his eyes not to blink.

"There's a lot of Frenchies by that name. I don't know no prison guard."

"I didn't say 'guard.'"

"I ain't ever seen you before, and you're telling me I been in prison."

"This man's brother was murdered by these two convicts. He believes one of them may have been shot. You limp when you walk, don't you?"

"I been limping since my horse hit a whistle-pig hole and throwed me over his head. Look at his hoof. It's splayed. He ain't going to be worth nothing to you."

"Take off your pants."

"What?"

"Take them off."

"You must be drinking the same stuff that drives these Indians crazy."

The lieutenant motioned to his sergeant major, who rode his horse forward out of the formation and kicked Son squarely in the middle of the face with his boot heel. He felt the Spanish roweled spur bite into his forehead, and he fell sprawling in the red dust, his nose ringing with pain. Two other enlisted men dismounted, pulled his boots from his feet, then began jerking his trousers off his legs. He kicked at them while they dragged him on his back, but he kept one arm pinned across the shirt that covered the wound in his side.

"Get up," the lieutenant said.

He rose to his feet and felt the wind blowing across his buttocks and genitals. The fat women by the venison racks were laughing in their hands, and he saw the eyes of the soldiers looking at his sex. The backs of his legs were shaking, and his hands were like wood by his sides.

'Turn around,' the lieutenant said.

"You greaser sonofabitch. Them Texians are going to cut your liver out one day, and I hope I'm there for it."

He saw the insult, the word, tick in the officer's eyes.

"You ought not to done that, Lieutenant," Hugh said. "You can see he ain't never been shot."

"Yes, but he's been whipped."

"Upbringing in the Cumberland Mountains ain't easy sometimes," Hugh said.

"I want both of you to leave this village. Don't ever come again," the lieutenant said. Then he turned toward Son and looked at him with a face as cool and smooth as marble. "Don't ever use words like that to a Mexican officer again. Today you are a fortunate young man."

The sergeant major brought up his horse, a Morgan with wideset eyes, and the lieutenant swung up into the split-wood saddle as though his body had no weight. Son watched him post ahead of the formation and the two long strings of Indian horses that followed him toward the pine trees.

He picked up his pants and put them on awkwardly. He felt as though he were moving inside a dream. For the first time, he looked back at the tepee and saw that White-Man's-Woman had gone inside and tied the flap to the lodge pole.

"I seen actors on stage in a public house that never done that good," Hugh said.

"I wasn't doing no acting."

"Hell, you wasn't. I thought any minute your side was going to pop loose and spill jelly all over that lieutenant's boot."

"I'm going to get a dirk in that fellow, Hugh."

"No, you ain't."

"He earned a new asshole today."

"The only thing you and me are going to do is get our butts out of here. I wish that Mexican had said how long ago he seen Emile Landry. Maybe he figured we headed toward Bexar or the coast, but the chances are he knows we didn't get too far with you carrying a ball. I'd feel a lot better if we got a big piece of Texas between us and him."

"He probably went on through. There must be money on us now, and that Mexican would have taken us with him if he thought he could turn a dollar on our hides."

"Emile Landry is just smart enough to let us think like that, too. He might be a cruel sonofabitch, but he can sniff a blood spore in the ground like a dog. Before they sent you up to the camp, a crazy fellow got loose from the chain once and ran back through the marsh. All the other guards figured he'd just die in there because he was so crazy he couldn't poke a hand in his mouth to feed himself sometimes. But Landry went after him and brought him back on a rope behind his horse."

"That don't change nothing. I still want a piece of that Mexican."

"I don't like to tell you things all the time, but what you let get done to yourself out here saved us from going back to the pen. If it had been me when I was your age, I would have cut that fellow from his belly button right up to his throat. And that's how I spent all the years I did in Frenchy jails. It ain't good to look back sometimes and figure how many years you lost because you didn't know how to stick a hot iron in water."

"Hugh, if you ain't slick as wheel grease."

"I think you're starting to learn something. In fact, that's about the smartest thing you ever said. I'm right proud of you."

It began to rain softly that night, and inside the tepee they cooked a stew of the raccoons Hugh had killed and ate it from the clay bowls with their fingers. A few rain drops fell through the chimney and hissed on the hote stones around the fire, and Son could hear the wind beginning to blow more strongly in the pines. He lay under a buffalo robe with his head on a blanket and listened to Hugh's outrageous stories while the woman slept on the opposite side of the fire.

"I don't give a damn if you believe me or not," Hugh said. "I knowed Dan'l Boone. Me and my daddy met him at a place called Bean's Station in Tennessee when he was an old man."

"What kind of work did your daddy do?"

"He was good at doing things wrong. It was a talent with him. He was so good at it that people would find out how he done something and then turn it around when they done it themselves. He dug water wells on high ground, planted his seed just before

a storm, built the smokehouse next to the bedroom, hired a drunkard to run his still, penned his hogs in a hollow that flooded each
year, put lye-water on infected warts, and set fire to his own beard
every time he lit his pipe."

Son felt his face begin to glow with sleep and the warmth of
the fire, then he heard Hugh's voice faintly above the rain and the
wind in the trees. In a bright corner of his mind he saw the pine
logs flare briefly and crumble into ash.

He didn't know how long he had been asleep when he heard
the tepee flap open and felt a spray of rain across his face. Iron
Jacket stooped his head as he came inside, and behind him a
streak of lightning jumped across the black sky. His wet hair was
unbraided, and he wore a Mexican enlisted man's coat with the
sleeves cut off at the shoulders.

"Close the flap, Iron Jacket," Hugh said. "I ain't fond of sleeping
in the mud."

"The old man comes," the Indian said.

"What is it?" Hugh said.

"Come to tepee."

"Are them Mexicans back?"

"You talk with me."

"Just say what it is. I ain't going out in that rain."

The Indian looked at him with his flat hazel eyes.

"No more talk here," he said.

"You're right, Son," Hugh said, as he put on his boots. "There's
crazy people everywhere these days."

Son tied the flap to the lodge pole again after Hugh and Iron
Jacket stepped out into the rain. The shallow red ditch around the
edge of the tepee was almost filled with water. He looked across
the dead fire and saw the woman's outline move under the blankets.

"What's that about?" he said.

She didn't answer, and he picked up a small pine cone and threw
it in her direction.

"Don't let on like you're asleep," he said. "You people can hear
a frog hop while you're sleeping."

"The Mexicans shamed Iron Jacket in front of the village."

"I don't know how you can shame an old thief like that. It sure
didn't bother him none when he pointed us out to that lieutenant."

"He's leader of the Choctaws because he always has food and clothes for the people. With no horses to sell back to the Americans, we will have no food when the brown moon is finished."

"What do you mean you won't have no food? These woods is full of deer and everything else."

"The Choctaws are not real hunters. They fish—back across the river where the Americans come from. The Mexicans make Iron Jacket a warrior in front of the village because he steals for them. They give him the buffalo robes they trade from the white hunters. Now the Choctaws will have nothing."

"You still ain't answered my question. What's that old sonofabitch got in mind for Hugh and me?"

"Bad."

"You're a regular blabber mouth, ain't you? What's he going to do? Tell the Mexicans I caught a ball in my side?"

"He wears the iron shirt to make the people believe he's a warrior. But he sends others to fight and steal for him."

Hugh unfastened the thong on the tepee flap and stooped inside with a muddy blanket over his head. Water dripped out of the tangle of hair over his eyes.

"Get that fire started again. You won't believe what that dumb bastard wants to do," he said.

"He wants to get even with a bunch of Mexicans tonight." Son picked up a handful of dry pine needles and rotted twigs and placed them on top of the flat cook-stone in the center of the fire pit. He begun striking two pieces of flint into the edge of the needles.

"How did you know that?"

"I just guessed. In fact, let me guess a little more. He wants to burn their stockade down, but he'd like us to do it."

"He ain't that dumb, and I ain't, either. I didn't know it, but that lieutenant really stuck a bayonet up his ass out there today. The only reason these Choctaws follow Iron Jacket around is because nobody ever goes hungry or gets cold while he's taking care of them with the Mexicans. But right now he ain't worth a wad of spit with his people."

Son watched the pine needles catch slowly, and he fanned the sparks into the kindling.

"So what are we going to do?" he said.

"He wants to steal all them horses back tonight, and any others they got, besides."

"And you said we'd go."

"Damn right, I did. He's going to raid their herd, anyway, and when he gets done we better not be around here."

"I don't want to offer no problem, but what are we going to ride?"

"You can't wait to start asking questions, can you? Like I'm some old fool that don't know how to take a squat by himself. He's got six horses hid out in the trees that he was going to sell to the Texians on his own. The Mexicans keep all their herd in a meadow about two miles south of their stockade, and they don't leave more than three or four pickets on guard at night. When we hit the herd, his people are going to fold up everything and head for the Brazos. They figure they can't do no worse there than what that lieutenant's been doing to them around here."

The fire flared and lighted the inside of the tepee. Son could see the dark spots of rain on the stitched deer skins.

"What do we get out of it besides a couple of mounts?" he said.

"I told him I wanted at least eight head. We can run them between us without no trouble, and we'll sell them off to a trader I know the other side of the Trinity. What do you think?"

"It's not as good as raising that lieutenant's belly button a few inches, but it'll have to do."

"All right, that's it, then. We're going to see Jim Bowie, and we'll have some hard dollars in our pocket when we do."

The woman hit Hugh on his sleeve with her fingertips. The firelight wavered on her face.

"I go with you," she said.

"Wait a minute," Son said.

"I don't belong to Iron Jacket's women again."

The pine cones snapped in the fire pit, and Hugh looked steadily at Son.

"It's going to be tough for her if she has to go back with them fat squaws again," Hugh said.

"Emile Landry is out there somewhere. You said it yourself. We got to move our ass across a big piece of country."

"I ain't arguing one way or the other. It don't make no difference to me. I just said them squaws are going to treat her like sheep flop when she starts toting and fetching for them again."

"Damn you, Hugh."

"Make up your own mind about it. Don't put them things on me."

"I give you something," she said. "Buffalo Hump's rifle and the metal balls and the horn with the fire dust."

"Now, you see, there wasn't no decision at all," Hugh said. "Where's it at?"

"His woman put it in the ground by the spring in the trees after they killed him. Then she went back toward where the Americans come from."

Outside, they heard horses' hooves splashing in the mud.

"Let's get it," Hugh said. "Does she go with us or not?"

"I didn't say she couldn't, did I? Why don't you stop all them tricks of yours?"

They stepped out into the rain and saw the women of the village taking down the tepees and rolling the deer skins and buffalo robes into tight bundles that they tied onto the tops of travoises with strips of hide. The rain drove through the skeletal frames of lodge poles and hissed in the fire pits. Iron Jacket and three other Indians sat bareback on their horses with bows and quivers of arrows over their arms. Iron Jacket wore his mail vest under his Mexican enlisted man's coat, and he and the other Indians had streaked their faces with a mixture of blackberry juice and animal fat. They all wore buckskin breeches, and their legs clung to the sides of their horses as though they had been welded there.

The woman stepped out last from the tepee.

"White-Man's-Woman no go," Iron Jacket said.

"We took a vote on that," Hugh said. "We decided we need somebody to keep on cooking for us and dressing out our game and such as that."

"Woman no go on raid against Mexicans."

"Now, you give us her as part of the deal for our horses," Hugh said. "You sharped us a little bit on that trade, and I don't want to lose what we got."

"Only six horses. She stay with women."

"We ain't going to argue about it," Son said. "She comes along, or you can go up against them Mexicans on your own."

"*Tonto* boy," Iron Jacket said. He motioned to one of the Indians behind him, who brought up two unshod, unsaddled horses by their bridles.

Hugh and Son pulled the reins back over the horses' ears and slid up on their backs. The rainwater was cutting deep rivulets through the red clay earth in the center of the village. A white spiderweb of lightning broke across the sky, and the horses spooked sideways in the mud.

Son sawed back the bit and put his hand down toward the woman.

"Get on up here. Let's find that rifle," he said.

They rode at a walk across the clearing into the trees, while the Indian women finished loading everything that was of any worth to them on the travoises—jerked venison, scalded and salted piglets and dogs, clay bowls filled with flint arrow points, turkey feathers stiff with animal grease for arrow shafts. Only once before had Son seen an Indian village move so quickly, and that was in Tennessee when they heard that the white man's fever, smallpox, had been found west of Cumberland Gap.

The rain dripped out of the pine trees in large flat drops that made the horses blink their eyes and toss their heads against the reins. The woman held Son around the waist, and he could smell smoke in her hair and that odor of fleshed-out raccoon hide in her clothes.

"You ain't got to hold on like that," he said. "These Indian horses can go through a woods at night like an owl."

They were following the stream that led up through the piney woods to the Mexican fort, and just before the stream made a bend back through an outcropping of rock dripping with moss and fern, the woman pointed at a streak of water leaking through the roots of the pine trees high up on the embankment.

"There," she said. "Under the rocks by the spring."

Son reined the horse, and he and the woman walked up the rise to where the spring water glistened along the ground. Ahead, Iron Jacket and the other three Indians stopped their horses and turned them around in the stream.

"You come," Iron Jacket said.

"Tell them to go on. We'll catch up," Son said.

"You tell him. I got a notion he might want that rifle," Hugh said.

"He ain't getting it."

"Come now. Moon no pass when we take horses," Iron Jacket said.

Son ignored him and began lifting a pile of flat stones that covered an eroded rock opening in the embankment.

"That rifle better be there, or them Indians are going to think you're really crazy," Hugh said.

The woman reached inside the opening and pulled out a long object wrapped in deer skin and tied with thongs. The thongs had dried and drawn tight as wire, and even with his teeth Son couldn't loosen the knots.

"You're going to be eating with your gums, boy," Hugh said, and flipped his knife underhanded up the embankment.

Son unrolled the deer skin from the rifle, and then he saw the long barrel and the tapered stock and the flintlock action.

"A Kentucky," he said.

Even though in the dark he couldn't see every detail of the rifle, he already knew each piece of it from memory as well as an ancestral mountain veneration for the weapon that Daniel Boone and his men had carried. He knew the wood was maple or apple and had been wrapped with tarred twine which the gunsmith burned away to give the stock grain. The bore was rifled so that the ball would drop only three inches in one hundred yards, and the balance was so perfect under the trigger guard that just the removal of the split-hickory ramrod under the barrel would upset it. He cocked back the hammer and opened the flashpan and ran his thumb along the smoothness of the steel. No water or rust had gotten to it, and the sides of the octagon barrel were as slick as when they had been honed in the smithy's vice.

"Look at it, Hugh. My uncle owned one, and he could knock a turkey's eye out at fifty yards with it."

"It ain't worth a shit to you tonight unless you got the rest of it," Hugh said.

Son propped the half-moon brass butt piece of the stock on his thigh and flipped open the rest of the deer skin. Inside the folds was a powder horn with a beveled wood plug at the bottom and a smaller one in the loading end. He hung the horn across his chest by its thong and unsnapped the cover on the elongated brass box set in the rifle's stock. He touched his fingers along the .45

caliber balls and the greased cloth patches that were used to slide them down the barrel and seal them tightly over the powder.

"It's like White-Man's-Woman said. It's all here," Son said.

"That not my name," she said.

He looked at her strangely in the flicker of lightning through the tree tops. Her eye with the small white scar in the corner, like a piece of string, was pinched at him in the drip of rain from the low pine limbs over their heads.

"You never told us your name," he said.

"Get it down here, Son," Hugh said. "Iron Jacket is fixing to blow a brown hole in his britches."

It had stopped raining when they rode out of the creek bed into the perimeter of woods that bordered the meadow where the Mexicans kept their horses. The night was still dark, with a crack of moonlight between the clouds, and a thick low fog floated in pools over the knee-high grass. The horses were penned in a one-rail corral, and two soldiers sat by a fire under a sheet of canvas stretched on poles. Son's horse began to nicker, and he leaned forward with the rifle balanced on his thigh and cupped his hand over its nose.

"There must be a hundred head in there," Hugh whispered.

Son strained his eyes into the darkness and traced a line from one end of the corral to the other, in the same careful way that he used to move his vision across a stretch of woods when he was hunting deer back in the Cumberlands. Then he saw the soft outline of both mounted pickets by the far end of the fence.

"How do you want to take them?" he said.

"We get them all at one time," Hugh said. "Ain't that right, Iron Jacket? You let your bucks circle wide and bring down them two on horses, and we go right through the middle and stick the Kentucky up the noses of them other two. White-Man's-Woman keeps the horses and rides in when we whistle. How's that?"

"You use knife on Mexicans," Iron Jacket said.

"We're going to pig-string them two so they don't get loose till their own people finds them," Hugh said. "It's the same thing."

"We take coup this day," Iron Jacket said.

"You take care of your side of it," Hugh said. "Don't truck with what's ours."

"Take coup."

"I done told you, Iron Jacket. There ain't a sound coming out of them Mexicans. Now, don't be pestering folks about it."

"Old man with bad eye just like *tonto* boy. Fool."

Iron Jacket and his three braves dismounted and tethered their horses to pine saplings. They slipped their bows and quivers of arrows off their backs, inserted one arrow loosely in their bow strings, and put another in their teeth. The tallest of the three braves took a tomahawk out of his legging and stuck it down the back of his buckskin breeches. They moved out of the trees in a crouch and disappeared into the grass. Son looked hard at the pools of fog on the meadow and the wet tips of grass bending in the wind, but he could see nothing of the Indians' movement.

"Stop studying on them Indians," Hugh said. "What they do ain't no business of ours. Get your rifle loaded. I don't want to grow no older here."

Son pulled the wood plug from the powder horn with his teeth and poured into the barrel, then took a lead ball and a greased patch from the brass box set in the stock and ran them down to the charge with the ramrod. He poured the flashpan and closed its cover.

"How's your flint?" Hugh said.

"It ain't hardly worn."

"Let's get our peckers down in the dirt, then. Don't stand up out of the grass till you hear the Indians first."

"You said we all hit the Mexicans at the same time."

"Shit on that. If them Indians mess it up, they're on their own. You and me is going to be long gone."

They crawled on their stomachs and elbows through the wet grass with Son in front. He balanced the rifle in the crook of his arms and let the powder horn drag at his side. A gust of wind blew across the meadow and flattened the grass around them, and they froze with their faces in the damp earth. The barrel and the flash pan of his rifle glistened with water, and he wondered if his primer would still fire when the flint touched the steel. He could hear the Mexicans by the fire talking now, and he put his thumb over the heavy hammer and pulled it back to half-cock. The sound was like a thick dry twig snapped across someone's knee. He felt Hugh's fist hit him in the sole of the boot. He didn't have to look back to feel Hugh's livid anger at his stupidity.

They moved forward until they could see the wavering shadows of the fire through the grass. Hugh was next to him now with his knife in his hand. Their dry controlled breathing and the sweat rolling off their faces was an agony in the stillness.

Why don't them savages do their bloody work, he thought, and then he felt shame and guilt at what he knew he wanted in his fear.

You ain't no different than them red niggers, are you, he thought. You want their pickets cut open so you don't catch a ball when you jump them Mexicans by the fire.

He squinted through the grass and saw one soldier stand up in silhouette against the fire and begin to urinate in the darkness. Then he heard a loud voice in Spanish back by the horse pen and a murderous blow like stone crunching through an earth-filled clay pot.

"Get it!" Hugh shouted, and hit him violently in the shoulder with his elbow.

Son went to his feet and ran forward with his rifle pointed at the soldier who was still urinating into the wind and staring into the darkness over his shoulder at the same time.

"Both you fellows get on your face," he said. "You hear me? Lie down on the ground like you was a pair of lizards."

The soldier who was standing looked at him in disbelief, and the man seated by the fire started to raise his hands, then lowered them and finally began to shake all over.

"Get on your damn face," Son said. "I got a .45 ball in here that'll bust you all over the bushes."

The two soldiers' faces were terrified in the firelight, and the soldier who was still seated kicked his rifle and his leather powder flask away from himself.

"They don't talk English," Son said. "How do you tell them to lie down in Spanish?"

"You ain't got to. They're scared so bad now they couldn't button their britches."

Hugh walked to the fire and kicked at it until it flared into a large flame again. The sparks showered up into the canvas stretched on the poles overhead. Out in the darkness, they heard a man scream.

"What are they doing?" Son said.

"It ain't our business. We done our end of it, and we take the horses we got coming."

Son's hands were damp on the stock of the rifle, and he thought something was beginning to tremble inside him.

"Tell them to stop," he said, and the words seemed to click in his throat with a guilt that he knew he would not resolve easily.

"It stopped with that poor fellow's scream," Hugh said.

Iron Jacket and his three braves walked into the firelight leading the saddled horses of the Mexican pickets behind them. The tallest of the braves was spotted with blood, and the stone tomahawk pushed down in the front of his buckskin breeches had patches of human hair stuck to it.

"Two coup," Iron Jacket said, and held up the scalps in the yellow light of the fire. On one, there was still a piece of skull plate attached. "Now other two before men from soldiers' town come."

"We already been through that before, Iron Jacket," Hugh said. "This pair is ours."

"No leave Mexicans to tell."

"We ain't going to do it that way," Hugh said. "What we're going to do is divide up these horses, get across the Trinity, and drink a lot of whiskey."

"First, Mexicans," Iron Jacket said.

"Are you hard of hearing or something?" Son said. "We got eight head coming, or maybe more since there must be a hundred head out there, and the Mexicans get trussed up and that's it."

"No talk with young boy. Old man talk."

"You don't listen too good, do you?" Son said. "You done taken all the coup you're going to tonight."

The two soldiers, who now sat flat-legged in the dirt, began to realize that the continuation or the end of their lives was being decided in the wavering yellow light. The skin on their faces grew tight, and their eyes had the plaintive look of hurt animals.

"A deal's a deal, Iron Jacket," Hugh said. "Besides, he's the one holding the rifle."

"No use. Sweat on face with fear."

"You asshole," Son said, "You didn't take them scalps. You got

Slim here to do it for you. You open your mouth again to me like that and I'll give you a belly button you can put a pie plate through."

"He's a crazy enough sonofabitch to do it, too," Hugh said. "I don't have no truck with him when he's like this."

"Don't talk with him no more. Whistle up the woman," Son said.

"She's right behind you."

Son turned and saw White-Man's-Woman sitting on his horse with the reins of the other five in her hands. Her knees were drawn almost up to the horse's withers to hold him in.

"All right, let's get what's ours and pig-string the Mexicans and find that horse trader friend of yours," Son said.

"How about that, Iron Jacket?" Hugh said. "We're too damn rich to set here and piss on each other till the damn Mexicans come to relieve their pickets."

"You hang too when soldiers tell," Iron Jacket said.

"There isn't nobody hanging us. Especially not no Mexicans," Son said.

"Tell your braves to drop down the rick and cut out our horses," Hugh said. "The deal was eight and I hold by that, but we don't want none with a brand and no quarters or pintos."

The first gray edge of dawn broke along the bottom of the eastern sky, and the wind picked up out of the trees across the meadow. Son heard the Indians drop the rail off the fence into the grass and begin turning the herd into a circle. Hugh pulled down the canvas stretched on the poles over the fire and cut six long narrow strips out of it with his knife. The Mexicans still sat in the dirt with eyes like wounded deer.

"There isn't nothing going to happen to you," Hugh said. "We're going to tie you up so tight your eyeballs come out, but them Indians ain't going to bother you."

But they didn't understand, and they saw only the wide-blade knife in Hugh's hand.

"These are sure hopeless sonsofbitches, ain't they?" Hugh said. "I don't know why Sam Houston ain't run the bunch of them in the Gulf yet. Turn the short one over and knot his hands to his feet."

Son took two strips of wet canvas from Hugh's hand and touched the Mexican on the shoulder. The man's body shivered with fright under his fingertips.

"When you get done, take their guns and their ammunition boxes," Hugh said. He was seated atop the prone body of the other soldier, tying knots in the canvas strips that would turn to rock in the sunlight. "I want to make sure Iron Jacket don't try to slip in a couple of lame ones on us."

"You done good about the Mexicans, Hugh."

"When are you going to learn? I don't care about these bastards. When their relief gets here, they'll tell them we saved their lives and we ain't got but eight of their horses. They'll go after Iron Jacket and the rest of the herd."

"You always play every card in your hand, don't you?"

"You damn right. That's why me and you are going to be splashing across the Trinity while them Indians are shooting over their shoulders. And I sure wouldn't want to be them and get caught after bashing open them two pickets."

Hugh rose up from the soldier and walked to the collapsed pen, where the Indians were cutting out the stallions and haltering them in strings with the Mexicans' lariats. When they drove the whole herd westward, the mares would follow the stallions without a rope and could be controlled with only a few outriders. The sky was beginning to soften more rapidly now, and Son kept looking at the distant line of trees where he expected the pickets' relief to emerge at any moment.

He unfastened the belts on both soldiers and slid off the ammunition boxes and picked up their leather powder flasks. He put the boxes and flasks inside his shirt, and cocked back the hammers of their rifles in the firelight. The action was filled with dirt and grease, and the cap holes were corroded with burned powder. He slipped off the long tapered bayonets with the blood groove and threw them into the grass.

"I told you we didn't want none of them inbred pintos," he heard Hugh say.

"Hugh, it's getting awful light."

"Shit on that. We ain't driving no pintos twenty-five and thirty miles at a lick. They'll be walking on their knees before we get to the river. You understand that, Iron Jacket? That's clear enough, ain't it? You cut that dog food out of our string or me and you is going to get mad at each other."

The tall Indian with the bloody tomahawk stuck in his breeches pointed at the distant woods.

"Where?" Hugh said, as they all stared, momentarily frozen, in the same direction.

The tall Indian pulled a flint knife with a deer-antler handle from his legging and stuck it in the soft ground, then bent over it on all fours and clenched the handle in his teeth. The scalp lock braided on the back of his head glistened from the dew. He rose up quickly and spoke to Iron Jacket while moving his hands rapidly at the same time.

"Tell somebody else," Son said.

"He ain't got to. We're in the shit house," Hugh said. "Throw them Mexican rifles away and let's get the hell down the pike. This part of the country is wearing out for us in a hurry."

Hugh pulled their string of eight horses toward the fire while Son mounted one of the Indians' horses and galloped between the two terrified soldiers. He balanced the Kentucky rifle on his horse's withers and grasped the lariat from Hugh's hand.

Hugh was trying to mount his horse, which was swinging in a circle each time he tried to throw his weight over its back.

"Hold, you shit hog, or I'll fillet your nuts and feed them to you," he said. The horse's hooves kicked into the fire and covered the two soldiers with sparks and ash.

"Pull back the bit," Son said.

"What's it look like I'm doing? His mouth must have been trained on rusted wire."

The woman brought her horse next to Hugh's so it couldn't swing away from him again. He grabbed the mane in his fingers and swung up over the horse's rump, his walleye shining with effort.

"You got it?" Son said.

"Hell, I always got it. Did you get the money off the Mexicans?"

"What money?"

"That Mexican scrip. Do I have to tell you everything each time? Their enlisted men got wads of it stuffed down in their crotch. You stick one of them in the butt and they explode like turkey feathers."

"Look back of you," Son said. "There's about a dozen of them sonsofbitches coming out of the pines now."

"Oh shit, let's run for it, boy. We're too young to bounce off a tree."

The three of them raced their horses, with the roped string of eight between them, toward an arroyo that led up through the western side of the timber. The horses' hooves showered divots of grass and dirt over Son's body; and when he looked behind him he saw Iron Jacket and his braves trying to stampede the herd toward the far woods, but the stallions were still roped together and spooking back toward the pen, and the mares were turning in a circle and raking down the other fence rails. Then Son heard the popping of musket fire, and he was glad the Indians were between them and the Mexicans.

They hit the arroyo in a full gallop and whipped their horses up the incline. The pines were thickly spaced on each side of the ravine, and in moments the meadow was out of sight behind them. Rolling fields covered with mist in the soft morning light opened up before them, and as Son laid into his horse and felt the steady rhythm between his legs he thought he heard a man's scream in the distant spatter of musket fire.

FOUR

They rode for three days before they reached the Trinity River. The roots of the oaks and willows along the banks were exposed by the receding water, and sandbars gleamed in the current, but the river was still too high and swift to ford with the string of horses.

"Let's go north and look for a narrows," Son said.

They rode for a half day along the river's edge and still didn't find a crossing that wasn't filled with deep holes and tangles of brush and dead trees.

"Where's that ferry you told us about?" Son said.

"It was along here somewheres, unless the Mexicans burned it up."

"You want to turn out the string and swim it?"

"We ain't going to do that. That's gold dollars on the hoof. Let's keep going upriver. We'll find us something."

"We ain't exactly got all the time in the world."

"I don't figure they're still after us."

"How do you know that? Even riding the way we was we couldn't have gained more than a half day on them and we done shot that already."

"Them Mexicans take a nap every afternoon. They don't get up till somebody cuts a bean fart and tells them it's dinner time. They're way back yonder someplace."

"All right, we ride till last light, then cut the string and swim it. Fair enough?"

"We'll talk about it then. In the meantime you study on what it's going to be like coming out on the other side of the river. I'm talking about wore-out mounts, wet powder, and not a piece of money in your britches."

Ten miles farther up the river, when the red sun was just striking the tops of the oaks and willows on the far side, they saw the ferry moored in the shadow of a huge cypress. In their exhaustion they didn't wait for the ferry-keeper to come out of his cabin but rode their horses across the split-oak planks onto the barge. Son slid down from the buckskin he was riding and leaned his arms and head against the horse's withers.

"You don't have money for pay," the woman said. Her legs and clothes were spotted with the wet sand from the river bottom. Her face was drawn, the metallic complexion almost discolored like uneven bronze, and Son saw her flinch as she pulled her buttocks back on the horse's rump and drew her knees up on its side.

"Don't worry about it," Son said. "I'll give him a chunk of lead to chew on if he don't want nothing else."

"I not give you rifle for that."

"I ain't going to shoot nobody. We just ain't bargaining with none of these people."

"Hey, get your ass out here," Hugh shouted at the cabin. "We got people and stock on board here waiting to get taken across."

An old man with white whiskers and white hair hanging in knotted strands from under his flop hat stepped through the low cabin door and walked toward them with his back still bent. His face had the softness of a baby's, and even in the diminishing twilight Son could see the blue veins in his fish-white arms.

"I always yell at the wrong people," Hugh said.

The old man picked up a long shaved pole that was leaned into a branch of the cypress tree and squinted up at their silhouettes against the late sun's fire. His gums were pink and without a tooth.

"What you boys and this Indian woman going to give me for poling you across? I don't take no Mexican scrip," he said.

"We ain't got money of any kind," Son said. "We'll cut out that pinto for you."

"Wait a minute," Hugh said. "That's worth five American dollars across the river."

"What else we got to trade, Hugh?"

"Before you boys start arguing, them horses ain't worth shit to me," the old man said. "But if you're G.T.T.'s, which I figure you are, and you're fixing to join up with Sam Houston, you don't pay nothing for this trip."

The old man dropped the pine rail into place between the lashed posts on the stern and slipped the mooring line loose so the ferry could swing out into the current on the rope that extended across the river.

"Did them Mexicans do something pretty bad to you?" Hugh said.

"I come here as a colonist with Stephen Austin fourteen years ago. They throwed him in prison in Mexico City, and they been giving Americans hell ever since. The taxes you can't pay they take out of your larder or drive out of your pen. If that ain't enough for them, the *jefe* comes back and takes all the tools and harness out of your barn. Then they sell it to them drunk Indians that come over from Louisiana."

"To tell you on the square, mister," Hugh said, "we're G.T.T.s all right, but we ain't planning to sign on in no army. So maybe you still got your fare coming."

"If you boys stay in Texas, you'll join up with Houston or Bowie, one."

"You know James Bowie?" Hugh said.

"I taken all them boys across," the old man said.

"I mean you ferried Jim Bowie from Louisiana across this river?"

"All them people come across on this ferry." The old man's light blue eyes turned away toward the water with his lie.

"We're looking for a horse trader on the other side named Jack Tyler," Son said.

"I know where he's at," Hugh said.

"You ain't been here in years, Hugh. You don't know he's alive."

"He's alive, all right," the old man said. "You watch him, too. He'll sharp you out of the nails in your horse's shoe."

"How far?" Son said.

"I told you where it's at," Hugh said. "We catch the trace just beyond the next rise and ride about five miles. Ain't that right?"

"He ain't there no more," the old man said. "Some buffalo hunters didn't like his whiskey one night and burned him down. He's about ten miles further on now at a regular town."

"There ain't no town there," Hugh said.

"There sure as hell is. Jack Tyler's got a saloon and a couple of stock barns there, and two fellows from Tennessee built thcmselves a store."

The ferry bumped onto the mudflat under the overhang of trees, and the old man dropped the rail on the bow.

"What do you want for the trip? We don't ask for nothing free," Son said.

"You got what I want up there on the horse, but I done got too old for that."

Son looked away from the old man's face and avoided the woman's eyes, which he knew were upon him.

"Give him the knife," he said.

"You sure can give away what ain't yours," Hugh said.

"Give him the damn knife."

"You can have this gut ripper," Hugh said. "I lost the whetstone, but you put one to it and you can lop a young pine in half with it."

"You stick it in one of them Mexicans for me and we'll be even," the old man said.

"Suit yourself," Hugh said. "Tell me, you taken any Frenchmen across of recent?"

"Last week I did. Five of them. They was wearing coats and pantaloons like New Orleans dandies."

Son and Hugh looked at each other.

"What kind of business was these Frenchies on?" Hugh said.

"You got me. Only one of them talked English, and he was such a mean-looking sonofabitch I didn't care to hold no conversation."

"Was they headed up the trace?" Son said.

"If you're going across east Texas, there ain't no other way to go," the old man said.

They walked the string of horses off the ferry into the trees and rode up the embankment. The shadows around them were deep purple, like a bruise, and the last crack of red sun was burning into the western horizon.

"That's him, ain't it?" Son said.

"Maybe." Hugh was biting down on his lip and staring through the darkening trees.

"Who else comes through this country dressed like that?"

"I didn't reckon he'd get ahead of us. If he'd figured us right, he should have headed south for the Coast. That's what we ought to done, and he should have knowed it."

"The old man said they crossed last week. Maybe they pushed on to Bexar."

"It might be our luck they're setting at Jack Tyler's place waiting for us, too. Ain't this a slop jar full of it? I thought we'd be drinking whiskey tonight with Jack instead of sleeping in a cold woods again like a bunch of niggers."

"We can't take these horses no farther, anyway, Hugh. Let's bed down by that drainage."

"That sonofabitch must have sniffed every bush we pissed on since we swum across the Mississippi."

The wind blew across the river in a cold gust behind them and rattled pine cones along the ground.

"It's fixing to rain tonight," Son said. "We'll cut us a lean-to in them oaks and make a good fire. Tomorrow we'll decide if we ride into Tyler's place or cut bait and head south for Galveston."

"If I thought I knowed where that French asshole was right now, I'd turn it around on him and hunt his camp. I'd like to catch him and them other four asleep and give all of them a big red smile across their throats."

"That's what we need—murdering somebody in Texas."

"We stole horses, boy. They'll hang you faster for that over here than killing a man. Shit. I hate sleeping on the ground another night. Look at that sky. We're going to be floating in piss in the morning."

"Are you going to help us make a camp or complain the rest of the night?"

"You just do your share and don't worry about me. By morning, I'll be the one that gets us out of this." Then, because he had no other place to put his anger, he got down from his horse, stomped and kicked at the ground, hurled a rock crashing through the trees, and shouted at the top of his voice: "Landry, I'm going to fry your balls in a skillet."

It rained hard during the night, and the fire they built under the lean-to with the powder and flint from Son's rifle smoked and hissed in the damp air and then finally died. The blankets they had brought from the Indian camp were drenched and soaked with mud, and by dawn the three of them were shivering and miserable with cold. Son tried to find enough dry wood to start another fire and used up the rest of the powder in his horn without ever charring the kindling. They sat in the gray light, their bodies stiff and immobile in their wet clothes, and stared at the string of hobbled horses that were tearing at the grass in the mist.

"What do you want to do?" Son said.

"We ain't got no choice. It's more than a hundred miles to the coast, and we ain't even got powder for game now. We ride into Tyler's."

"We might go right back to the pen, too. If they don't blow us all over the street first."

"I ain't going back to prison, either, Son. There's another way."

The rain dropped out of the trees on top of the lean-to. Hugh pushed his wet hair back over his head and looked directly at Son.

"She goes in first," he said.

"Wait a minute."

"She goes in and finds out if any Frenchies are there."

"Hugh, that ain't right to send her in by herself."

"It's got to be that way. That ferry-keeper said they got a store there. Indians are always coming by to see a white man's store. It ain't nothing unnatural."

The woman was looking quickly at both of them.

"That saloon is probably full of drunk men, too," Son said.

"You come up with a better one, then. And while you're doing that, think about what happens to her if we get shot or put in shackles by Emile Landry. She's a long way from any Tonkawas, and there's people around here that would use her for a draft horse, if not worse. That includes Jack Tyler. If I know him, he's got a jenny-barn built out back of his saloon."

"It just don't feel right, Hugh."

"You spent two years in jail and you're stupid as the day you come in. I ain't doing nothing bad to her. I'm trying to keep the three of us alive. You remember she was in on that horse deal just like us."

Son flicked a twig at the ground.

"How long do we give her?" he said.

"The old man said it's about fifteen miles. We wait till tomorrow morning and then head for Galveston."

"No good," the woman said.

"Ain't you been listening?" Hugh said. "We ain't got a choice in the matter. There's people over here from Louisiana that will kill us or put us in a pen for the rest of our lives. Now, we taken you away from them Choctaws, and I reckon you owe us something."

"Damn, Hugh."

"Don't make me out the bastard. You know I'm right."

"I don't have the round metal to go into the store," she said.

"What?" Hugh said.

"She don't have any money. What's she supposed to do? Walk in and start asking if there's any Louisiana Frenchies around?"

"All right, you do this. Go to the saloon and ask for Jack Tyler. You won't have no trouble finding him. He never gets no further from his whiskey than a glass away. You just tell him that Hugh Allison wants to know if he can get credit at the bar. Now, you say my name back to me."

"I know your name."

"Say it."

"That's enough, Hugh."

"Hell, it is. All we got to do is step in our own flop just once today, and you and me is going to be in a jail wagon again."

"She understands."

"Well, that's what I'm talking about. I don't want no misunderstandings."

"I'll unhobble the gelding," Son said to the woman. "He ain't fast, but he's got a lot more stay to him."

He walked out under the dripping trees with the woman and slipped the bridle off her horse and put it on the gelding.

"You ain't actually got to go in that saloon," he said. "Maybe just go down to the horse pen and ask the hostler if there's a Frenchman around. Tell him a Mexican officer back east of the Trinity sent you."

"You stay till tomorrow," she said.

"We got to go if you ain't back by then. What Hugh said is true. Them men want to put us back in prison."

She slipped up on the back of the gelding as though she were made of air.

"What you did to this bad man?"

"We killed his brother."

Her eyes wandered over his face, then fixed steadily into his. "Why?"

"We didn't go to do it, I guess, but—I don't know, I can't think real clear about it."

She bent low over the horse and moved it through the wet trees, then once she was out of the timber she brought her heels into its sides and whipped the reins across its neck. Son watched her become smaller and smaller as she disappeared like a dark cipher into the mist rolling across the distant meadow.

"You ever seen the buck kick the doe out of the woods when he knowed a hunter was out there?" Son said.

"I don't want to listen to no more of it. You got too much a way of going along with what I say and giving me hell about it at the same time. You didn't hear her holler none. An Indian knows what's got to be done and keeps her mouth shut about it."

"Where you going?"

"To follow behind her. Use your head. There ain't no sense in shivering here all day and waiting for her to ride back the whole fifteen miles."

By noon the sunlight broke through the haze and dappled the soft green of the rolling hills. There were groves of live oaks and blackjack in the fields, and occasionally they saw mud-chinked log cabins with chimneys built of field stones. When they topped a hill, the country and the vast sky overhead seemed to reach endlessly to the western horizon.

"It's just big, ain't it?" Son said.

"Yes, it's enough country almost to make you give up being a criminal," Hugh said. "It's probably what Kentucky looked like when Dan'l Boone come in it. There wasn't nothing there except some Shawnees, and all you had to do was spit on the ground to make something grow."

"What do you reckon's going to happen to this revolution?"

"Who knows? I'd sure hate to come out on the wrong end of it, though. That general Santa Anna is supposed to be a sonofabitch. It wouldn't surprise me none if he fired every white town in Texas.

But then again Jim Bowie can take a real mean vengeance when he gets the blood up in his head."

"What do you know about Sam Houston?"

"I always heered he was a drunkard. They run him out of Tennessee when he was governor. They say he went over to live with the Indians in Arkansas and stayed so drunk all the time he wasn't hardly human no more."

"How's he run an army?"

"From what I hear he's an old fox. He must be if Santa Anna ain't caught him yet and dropped him off a tree."

"Hugh, you ever think about putting it down in one place?"

"What?"

"I mean your own place. Not doing nothing for nobody else, just yourself."

"Anything I ever done was for myself. But what you're talking about is something else. That's why you come down the river to New Orleans. You had a notion of being one of them French dandies down at the cotton exchange. You seen what that got you. Them gentlemen in the courtroom put a little snuff up their nose and sent your ass to prison. The only place for the likes of us is rolling free so they can't get a chain on our leg. And that don't change no matter where you're at. Once this revolution is over, Texas won't be no different than back in the United States. They'll have a rule for everything and a manacle to go with it."

"You was in jail because you killed a man."

"But you wasn't. And I gone to prison before just like you. They should have hung me for what I done with the Harpes, but I always got in the worst trouble for stinking up the air around gentlemen. That's something Jim Bowie understood. When he come down to New Orleans he learned to dress and talk just like them. But they always knowed he'd slit their noses if they didn't address him proper."

Late that afternon they stopped their horses in a stand of oaks on a hilltop overlooking miles of meadowland. In the distance they could see where the trace disappeared into more trees and then a hazy line of green hills beyond.

"Tyler's place is probably beyond that next rise, ain't it?" Son said.

"I hope it is. My butt feels like somebody put a dirk up it."

"Five dollars a head, right? We're going to be rich if Landry ain't there."

"You watch out for Jack, though. He's got a way of putting it back in his purse."

"I don't plan on getting drunk on his corn or fooling with none of them jenny-barners."

"We need saddles, food, powder, and a shit pile of other things if we're going on to Bexar and don't want to keep looking like convicts. That shirt of yours smells like something died inside it. You might not know it, but living in an Indian camp gives you a stink that makes a white person's nose fall off, and that dried blood don't help it none."

"I'll be damned. Lookie yonder," Son said.

Hugh leaned forward on his horse and squinted with his walleye through the failing light.

"She must have poured it on that gelding," he said. "You see anybody behind her?"

"Not unless they're coming out of them trees."

"I got to admit: an Indian can get forty miles out of a horse when a white man can't get twenty. You sure you don't see nothing behind her?"

"There ain't nothing behind her except a shadow."

Five minutes later the woman walked the gelding into the oak trees. Its neck and flanks were covered with foam and its rib cage quivered under the touch of her heels. The woman's face was drained with exhaustion, and perspiration rolled in drops out of her black hair. She pushed herself back on the gelding's rump and dropped the knotted reins on its neck. Her exposed thighs were shaking.

"What'd Jack say?" Hugh asked.

"You can drink at the saloon all night on credit."

"He didn't see no Frenchmen there?" Hugh said.

"He say you come in and drink."

"Was there any foreign-looking people around? Men that look like they don't belong around here?"

"She done told you, Hugh. Don't talk to her like she's a child."

"Well, shit then, our luck has changed in another direction. I'm going to buy you all a supper tonight that would make the king of England piss in his slippers. I can't believe we got a chance to be free white people again."

It was dusk when they reached the settlement, and the cold twilight lay in a purple band on the rolling horizon. The road that led between Jack Tyler's saloon and stock barns and a store on the opposite side was scarred with wagon and horse tracks, and there were at least a dozen horses tethered in front of the saloon. Son's eyes moved over each saddle and gum coat or blanket roll tied across the horses' rumps.

"You see anything that don't smell right?" he said.

"None of them saddles is French. Quit worrying," Hugh said.

The saloon was built of split and notched logs with a raised porch, and the shuttered windows glowed with the yellow light of the oil lamps inside.

"I wish I had a load in this rifle," Son said.

"They wouldn't try to arrest us in there, nohow. I bet most of the boys drinking in there are Tennessee and Kentucky, and they ain't going to let a bunch of Frenchies arrest nobody in their place."

The two of them slipped off their horses and stepped up on the porch, but the woman stayed behind.

"Come on," Son said.

"The Americans don't want Indians," she said.

"You was in here this afternoon, wasn't you?" Hugh said. "They ain't going to eat you."

"I wait."

"No, you ain't," Son said, and took her by the arm and led her with him.

They pushed open the oak door and stepped into the heavy warmth of the room and the smell of stale tobacco smoke, wine, raw whiskey, and men's bodies. A fire was burning in a hearth made of field stones, and a black pot filled with chicken stew was boiling in the center of the logs. The long square tables were filled with men dressed in animal skins or colorless sweat-faded eastern clothes. Their unshaved faces were red with windburn and alcohol, and many of them wore pistols or knives on their chests. Son felt strange at being around so many white people who were not convicts. Then he noticed the women at the tables.

He had never seen women in a saloon before, except in New

Orleans and they were mulattoes. But these were white and Mexican women, and they were as drunk as the men with them. His father, who had been a religious man, once told him about a saloon in Nashville that had jenny-barners working in it, and his father had said he hoped Son would never allow his body to be corrupted by women who had Satan's diseases inside them.

A Mexican woman in a dirty white blouse with snuff stains on her lips sat on a hogshead behind the long plank that served as a counter.

"Where's Jack Tyler at?" Hugh said, loudly.

"In the back," she said.

"Tell him to get his dirty bum out here. My name is Hugh Allison, and I want three cups of that wine you're setting on."

"Fifteen American cents for each cup," she said.

"You just serve it up and get Jack."

"Fifteen cents for each."

"I ain't going to have to go around there and serve myself, am I? You put it right here on the board and tell that old sonofabitch to haul it out here."

"Slow it down," Son said, and leaned his rifle against the plank. He looked around at the men who were now watching the three of them.

"Ah, now there's our wine. I thank you, ma'am, because this is surely a gentleman's cup. Once, Jim Bowie and me and two other fellows from Kentucky drank a whole cask of this down on Congo Square in New Orleans. We got so drunk we set a cotton bale on fire, and Jim was going to roast one of them Frenchy gendarmes for breakfast."

The Mexican woman had disappeared behind the burlap curtain at the back of the room. The men at the tables had stopped talking and were looking intently at Hugh.

"You know James Bowie, mister?" One man said. He wore a gray flop hat over an enormous head, and his hands looked like frying pans. There was a large knife and a cap and ball pistol in a double holster on his chest.

"I knowed Jim for years. I knowed both of his brothers, too, when the three of them bought out most of the cotton exchange in New Orleans."

"Then if you know so damn much, what do you think about a

Texian that marries into Santa Anna's family?" the man said. His eyes were black and dilated with whiskey, and his body had the heavy, confident proportions of a man who knew he could command a room's attention simply by changing the tone of his voice.

Hugh sipped out of his cup and squinted his shining walleye at the men staring at him from the tables. Son moved his hand over to the rifle barrel and looked backward at the oak door.

"From what I understand James Bowie and Sam Houston is about to tear Santa Anna's nuts out," Hugh said. "I also understand that James Bowie would use that knife of his to slip the head off a drunk man that made a remark about his marriage. That probably don't apply here, but I'd sure hate to tell him about it when I get to Bexar. What's your name, anyway, mister?"

The pot of chicken stew cooking in the logs boiled over and snapped in the flames. The men at the tables went to fixing their pipes or motioning quietly to the Mexican woman to fill their cups again.

"It's all right that you don't remember your name, mister," Hugh said. "Sometimes a man gets his tongue caught in his cup and don't know how to speak right. Damn, if that ain't old Jack Tyler walking out with his britches unbuttoned."

Jack Tyler came through the burlap curtain at the far end of the plank. He couldn't have been over five feet tall, Son thought, and his hair hung on his wide shoulders like a girl's. His shirt sleeves and long underwear were rolled, and his stubby arms were knotted with muscle. There was a line of dead skin where his hat fitted his head, and Son could smell the corn whiskey and tobacco juice on his breath like a rancid odor corked in a stone crock.

"Ain't you got no shame, Jack? Why don't you button it up before it catches cold?" Hugh said.

"It's been a hell of a long time, Hugh," he said. "From what I heered about you, I didn't think you'd ever be over this way again."

"I always figured to come back to Texas eventually. New Orleans is all right, but the likes of me can't make no money there and I understand you all been having more fun shooting at Mexicans than hogs rolling in shit."

"Dealing with them sonsofbitches ain't exactly fun."

"Don't poor-mouth me, Jack. You'd make money selling sand to a thirsty man in a desert. Look, this here is Son Holland, a friend of mine from Tennessee, and this is White-Man's-Woman. We stayed a bit with the Indians back toward the Sabine."

Son put out his hand, and Tyler shook it as though he were momentarily picking up something strange and unfamiliar.

"You got something dead inside that shirt of yours?" he said.

"What do you mean?" Son said.

"You fellows must have been eating dog with them Indians," Tyler said.

"Maybe it's just where I'm standing," Son said. "The air smells right rank to me, too."

"The reason we stopped here, Jack, is to do some trading," Hugh said.

"I know the reason you stopped here, and we better go in back to talk about it."

"I ain't talking about nothing right now except money and some of that chicken stew and a lot of wine," Hugh said.

"We got time for that, but you all had better walk in back with me."

Son finished his cup and set it on the plank.

"I think he's got some news for us we don't want to hear," he said.

The three of them followed Tyler through the curtain into a back room with a dirt floor and a log ceiling. A plank table was nailed to the top of a sawed-off oak stump with an oil lamp on it and in the dim yellow light Son saw a fat Mexican woman lying on a bunk bed. Her stomach brought her dress over her knees, and there were rings of fat on her thighs.

"*Vaya por la comida y vino,*" Tyler said, then pushed the woman in the rear with his boot.

"Jack, your taste in a bunkie has sure changed. You used to be chasing the young ones around. Maybe we're getting too damn old for anything except them big sows, and that's what I wanted to talk with you about. What's the toll on them lady-fairs out there?"

"You better get serious for a space," Tyler said. "You and your friend from Tennessee ain't over here to shoot at no Mexicans. Four days ago a bunch of Frenchies come through here, and they had papers on both of you. I don't read no French and I couldn't hardly understand the head sonofabitch, but it looked to me like you all killed a prison guard."

"It's hard getting out of them Louisiana jails sometimes, Jack," Hugh said. "Then again, you can't always believe what a Frenchie will tell you."

The Mexican woman brought three plates of chicken stew with wooden spoons to the table, and a large green bottle of wine in a wicker cask.

"I ain't telling you what to do," Tyler said. "But that head fellow was a mean bastard, and I wouldn't want him after me."

"Where did they head?" Son said.

"West, down the trace, but that don't mean nothing," Tyler said. "Did you all really kill a prison guard back in Louisiana?"

"We killed that fellow's brother," Son said, and lifted a spoonful of the chicken stew into his mouth. The taste of cooked meat that wasn't game or boiled dog made him weak inside.

"What the hell are you going to do now?" Tyler said.

"After you sharp us out of the horses we got outside, we're going to Bexar and see ole Jim Bowie," Hugh said. His mouth was filled with food, and wine dripped out of his whiskers.

"Do you know what's going on over there?" Tyler said.

"What?" Son said.

"Ben Milam says he's going to kick all the Mexicans out of there and make it the capital of a new republic."

"Who's Ben Milam?" Son said.

"You ought to know that, boy, if you're fixing to join up with him," Tyler said. "He's from back in Kentucky, and he's a crazier sonofabitch than Bowie or Houston, both."

"Who you putting in with on this deal, anyway?" Hugh said.

"Anybody that can cut us loose from the Mexicans. But I don't think any of them fellows we got right now is going to help us. They say Sam Houston is drunk half the time, and Jim Bowie has been too close to Santa Anna to suit me. Stephen Austin claims he's general of the Texas army, but there ain't no army, except the volunteers they try to hold together from one day to the next. I'd like one Mexican rifle ball to fly across the Sabine so Andy Jackson's soldiers could come in and take over the whole damn country."

"Andy Jackson wouldn't do shit for none of us," Hugh said. His jaw was becoming slack with drink, and there was a fine bead of light in his walleye. He lifted his cup again and drank it to the bottom. "You know that. You was at Chalmette, too. We killed them redcoats by the hundreds. We drilled them right in the midle of their silver breast buckles while they marched into us with the sun in their eyes and the bagpipes playing their death song behind them. Then we run them with pig-stickers from the mudworks all the way back to the Gulf. What did Andy Jackson give us for it, or the ball I caught in my leg? Not enough scrip to buy two quarts of rum in New Orleans."

"It don't matter. Anything is better than living under these arrogant greasers," Tyler said.

"We want to trade that string we got out front," Son said. "You want to take a look at them?"

"I reckon you got a bill of sale on all of them, ain't you?" Tyler said.

"We got the same kind you probably got on some of them horses in your lot," Son said.

"The Mexicans is rough on me sometimes," Tyler said. "They come by and check my lot every couple of weeks, and they take anything I ain't got a paper on."

"We ain't trying to bargain with you," Son said. "Just look at the string, and we'll take half the amount in American money and the rest in trade."

"This is part of Mexico, boy, and you deal in Mexican money here."

"If you want to talk to me, my name is Holland, and that woman out at the plank wasn't taking no Mexican money for the drinks."

"You got a real pistol for a partner," Tyler said to Hugh.

"I got to admit I told him you're a bit of a sharper, Jack. But go look at them horses. They're a good string. They ain't branded or shoed, and you got many an Indian pony just like them. You and me both know the Mexicans ain't going to give you no trouble over them."

"What do you need in goods?" Tyler said.

"Everything, including a new shirt for Son."

"All right, you set here and I'll be back. Holler at the woman if you want more from the pot."

Tyler went back through the burlap curtain.

"You sure pick some mangy bastards for friends," Son said.

"He is a little rank sometimes, but he's still a friend. Don't forget we'd be between a rock and a hard place if he wasn't here."

"What do you reckon he'll offer on the horses?"

"Anything he can get away with. But figure it this way: an hour ago we didn't have nothing between us except an empty rifle and some spent horses that ain't worth their hides, and right now we're eating his food and drinking his wine. Pass that cask over here again. I believe he put a whole block of salt in that stew."

"You're into your cup, Hugh, you got your mind on them women out there, and if you let him sharp us on this deal we're going our different ways on the trace tomorrow."

"Now, that's a bad thing to say to a partner, ain't it, White-Man's-Woman?"

"I not White-Man's-Woman," she said. In the light from the oil lamp on the plank table her face looked as though it were cut out of mahogany. She held the wooden spoon balanced over the plate in her whole hand.

"Well, we ain't got anything else to call you," Hugh said. "I was just saying Son shouldn't be rough on his partner."

"You want bad women outside," she said. "They take your round metal and give you sickness back for it."

Hugh wiped the wine out of his whiskers with his hand, and poured again out of the cask.

"If this ain't something," he said. "A man spends three years locked in a pen, and when he gets out he's got a couple of church deacons for company. You just take care of yourselves. I was through this country in 1821 when an Indian would put an arrow shaft through your back as soon as he caught you sleeping in the saddle."

Hugh hit his hand on the table and knocked his plate into his lap. He stared at it blindly, then raked it with his palm onto the dirt floor.

"We're going to need a block and tackle to get you on a horse tomorrow," Son said.

"The last time I seen a block and tackle we was doing something else with it," Hugh said. He raised his cup to his mouth and spilled most of it down his shirt front.

Jack Tyler came through the burlap curtain with a leather purse in one hand and a large holstered pistol in the other. He looked at Hugh, whose face was white and vacuous as he stared at the green neck of the wine cask.

"That's a right fine string you got out there," he said. "I'll give you fifteen dollars American, the tack for two horses, all the grub and clothes you need, a dress for the woman, and I'll throw in something extra you ain't ever seen before."

"Wait a minute, mister. That's forty dollars worth of horses out there," Son said.

"You said you wanted it in goods as well as money, Holland. I'm giving you the best deal you'll catch between here and some Mexican trader up the trace."

"You said saddles for only two horses," Son said.

"An Indian don't ride a saddle," Tyler said.

"Three saddles, Jack," Hugh said. "We don't want no army ass-busters, either."

"All right," Tyler said.

"Hell, it is. You're trying to sharp your friend when he's got his head in the jug," Hugh said.

"You look here at what I got in this holster," Tyler said. "I reckon you heered about them, but you ever seen one before?"

"No, I ain't. It's a big sonofabitch, though, ain't it? Will all them chambers really fire?"

"Sam Colt himself was through here about five months ago, and he left me this one for the bill he owed at the bar," Tyler said. "We took it outside, and he knocked five slats out of my fence as fast as he could cock it."

Hugh picked up the heavy revolver in his hand, pulled back the hammer on half-cock, and rolled the cylinder across his palm.

"It looks to me like all them caps would light with the first flash," he said.

"You make up your own mind about it. I got all the powder and caps you need out front. Sam Colt said he figured out that turning chamber while he was carving a wood gun on board a navy ship."

"Before this goes on no further, let's make sure what we're going to get for our horses, Hugh," Son said. "We don't want no woman's dress, we don't want no salted fatback for grub, and no bill in the morning for what you're fixing to do tonight."

"You all talk about it. I'm going to find some real company," Hugh said.

"Damn you, it's coming out of your share if you have to go hungry down the trace," Son said.

Hugh careened through the curtain into the front room.

"Where can we sleep at?" Son said.

"I got some pallets fixed up in the back of the barn," Tyler said. "I'll send my Mexican woman over with some blankets. You want to take the bottle with you?"

"You can quit what you're thinking, because I ain't going to have liquor in my head when we count out our supplies tomorrow morning."

"You ought to take it with you."

"You just keep your dirty mouth to yourself, mister. And I'll take the pistol so Hugh don't forget what you already give him."

Son and the woman walked through the crowded front room toward the door. Hugh was at one of the long tables by the fireplace with a Mexican woman on each side of him. He was telling a story and crashing his fist down on the planks each time he finished a sentence.

It was cold outside, and the wind was blowing hard out of the north. The few stars in the blue-black sky were low over the dark hills, and leaves were shredding from the clumps of oaks in the fields.

"Ice fall from the sky in the morning," the woman said.

"What?"

"It comes from that star above the little hill."

"That's the end of the little dipper. It don't have anything to do with the weather. People at home say it means Jesus is showing you ain't got to reach up but just a little to see his plan."

"You see."

They went into the barn and walked between the stalls to the back, where hay had been piled and flattened under quilts beside one wall. In the darkness they could hear the wind ripping across the loft floor.

"I hate to think about the drunks that's going to be sleeping with us later," Son said.

"They stay all night in the saloon," she said.

"Hugh won't. They'll throw him out on his butt as soon as he's drunk enough to handle."

"He sleep with bad women tonight. He not come here."

Jack Tyler's fat Mexican woman came into the barn with an angle lamp and four folded U.S. army blankets. In the yellow flare off the lamp she looked awful. She dropped the blankets on the hay.

"No orinen por aquí," she said, then walked with her lamp through the stall while the horses knocked their hooves into the wood.

"What did she say?" Son said.

"She not want a squaw man and Indian woman in her barn."

"She didn't say that."

"How you know?" She unfolded one of the army blankets and lay down on the hay. "You think they like me here? How the Americans look at you when you walk out with me?"

"Those are all drunk men. Their heads are full of rut and whiskey. They wasn't paying no mind to us."

"Why you keep your hand so tight on pistol, then?"

He felt his face flush in the dark.

"Because I don't like dealing with a sharper like Jack Tyler," he said. "I don't like being in a saloon full of white trash and jenny-barners, either. Last, I put in a good day today and I don't feel like nobody holding me to the fire before I go to sleep."

He sat on a quilt and pulled off his boots. The hay sank under his weight, and a pain shot out of his rib cage into his heart that made his mouth go open for breath.

"Stay back," she said, and pressed her palms against his forehead.

He could smell the animal odor in her clothes again. She pulled his shirt back and touched her fingers along the scabbed wound in his side.

"You start bleed again," she said. Then she knelt beside him and began tearing away his shirt in strips.

"You crazy Tonkawa woman. That's the only shirt I got until Tyler gives me one in the morning, and Hugh's probably already drunk that up by this time."

"I wash. You wait," she said.

He watched her walk through the row of stalls, looking for a pail, then find one in a trough and push open the front door against the sky. He heard her release the winch on the well out in the lot and the hollow sound of the bucket hitting the water far below.

She washed his wound while he sat hunched with an army blanket over his shoulders.

"How'd you learn to talk English when you was with them Mexican buffalo hunters all the time?" he said.

"Mexicans not take me from the Tonkawas. Americans did. We were four women and seven children picking berries when they shoot everyone. They not kill me and my sister, but she die later. They take away my name Sana and call me White-Man's-Woman. Iron Jacket told you I was Tonkawa hand-blower. They not have that in my people. Later the Americans gave me to the Mexican hunters for the magic water and a gun."

"How'd your sister die?"

"She get the disease that lives in the water where the Comanches stay. It can live inside the Comanches and not hurt them because they are bad people, but it kill other Indians."

"Why'd you let Iron Jacket tell all them lies about you?"

"You and Hugh not ask me. You just listen to coward Indian."

"I'm listening now, ain't I?"

"You got bad feeling inside about Indians."

"That don't mean I don't like none of them."

"I hear you call them red niggers to Hugh. What they done to you that's so bad?"

"It don't make no difference now who done it."

"What they done?"

"Some drunk Shawnees killed my folks back in Tennessee."

"Who Shawnee?"

"I told you it don't make no difference. All them people is rubbed out, anyway. The only thing I got in my mind is getting away from Emile Landry. If Hugh don't stop getting careless, we're going to make a mistake and get sent back to the pen. They'll hang us when they get us back there, too."

"You strange boy. I never think you kill."

They heard voices rising in the saloon, then a crashing sound like a table being thrown on its side.

"Damn, I bet Hugh is back with the Harpe gang now," Son said.

"You not worry about him. He always know what he do."

"I think I remember one time he didn't and somebody went upside his head with a stick of firewood."

"You lie down now. Tomorrow you have new shirt."

"Tomorrow I'm going to be sobering up Hugh in the trough."

"He be all right. You lie down." She pressed him back on the pallet with her fingers. "You good boy. You live too much for so young."

He closed his eyes momentarily and smelled the hay and the odor of the horses in the stalls. The wind was rattling a piece of loose tack in the loft overhead. When he opened his eyes in the darkness again, he saw Sana lying on her hip next to him with her long hair folded into a curve under the blanket's edge.

Then between sleep and a dream, just before he was pulled away into the clicking of hailstones against the roof, he felt her lean over him, brush his forehead with her fingertips, and touch his mouth with hers.

It was bright and cold in the morning when Son walked out of the barn with an army blanket wrapped around him, and the hailstones had frozen in the horse lot like pieces of broken glass. Hugh was already up, tying their supplies down on a pack mule. His face was red in the wind, and he wore a flop hat pulled down low on his ears. He picked up a wool-lined canvas coat from the stack of supplies and threw it at Son.

"Put that on before you get the pneumonie," he said.

"I didn't reckon you'd be moving around this morning."

"The whiskey or wine ain't been made that can give me a hangover, boy."

"Let me get Sana and let's move it down the trace."

"Who?"

"That's her name."

Hugh grinned and pulled a leather thong into a tight knot.

"Don't say what's going on in that worthless mind of yours," Son said.

"I wouldn't dream of it. Don't walk off just yet. I done some late drinking and talking with Jack, and I think I got a couple of pretty good ideas. You remember what that ferry-tender said about hiding in the army? That ain't a bad notion. Besides, Jack said Sam Hous-

ton's promising six hundred and forty acres of land to any soldier
that'll see it to the end with him. You was talking about putting
it down in one place, and that's a hell of a lot of land to do it on."

"It don't look to me like he's going to have any land to give
out."

"Well, you take your chances when you play, don't you? And
once we're in the army, Emile Landry can't do shit to us."

"What's to stop him? Sam Houston don't represent no real government."

"You don't know nothing about soldiering on the losing side.
They ain't going to let nobody take you, because they need your
butt and musket there in the trench. It's the desperate people that
win the wars, boy."

"What about Sana?"

"I got that worked out. Jack says there's a Tonkawa camp over
on the Brazos. We leave her with her people and then head for
Bexar or wherever Sam Houston's at."

"Maybe she don't want to go back."

"Son, stop making it hard every time we got to do something.
We can't wander all over Texas with an Indian woman. Somewhere
along the line our luck is going to run out. The Mexicans are going
to get us, or Landry is, or maybe we'll just end up freezing to death
on the plains. When you're in a foul-smelling outhouse, you shit
through the hole and get out."

"You got a coat for her?"

"It's under them bags of jerky."

"I reckon I'm the one that tells her, too."

"That's up to you. But there ain't no two ways about it: she's got
a spark in her eye for you."

"I'll tell her on down the trace."

Hugh took a stub of a cigar from his shirt pocket and put it in
his teeth. He pulled the pack cinch tighter on the mule's belly and
looped it through the metal ring.

"If you want, I'll do it. She'll take it from me without no com-
plaint," he said. "What you don't understand about Indians is that
they don't fight against what they know they got to do. That's
why they don't have no fear in a battle."

"I'll talk with her. Don't say nothing."

"All right, let's get it, then. There's a woman inside that wants me to jump the broomstick with her. I don't know whether she's drunk or crazy."

"She probably just don't see too good."

They rode westward on the trace through the hills in the cold yellow sunshine, and at noon they ate a lunch of boiled coffee, jerked venison, and parched corn on the edge of a piney woods. Son had slipped the pack off the mule, and sat with his back against it and the barrel of the Kentucky rifle propped across his shin. The wind bent the grass to a pale green and yellow in the fields. Hugh had just lit another cigar he had gotten from Tyler's store when three men rode their horses out of the woods a hundred yards down from them. Son pulled the rifle up across his lap and snapped the hammer back to half-cock, and Hugh opened his coat and casually worked the Colt's revolver loose from his belt.

"Them three look like they fell out of a slop jar, don't they?" Son said.

"They're pretty mangy-looking, all right," Hugh said. "That one in front looks like somebody whipped his face with a thorn bush."

"Let's stop them where they're at."

"Let them come in. Maybe they just smelled our coffee."

The three riders were dressed in filthy deerskins, their breeches streaked with dung and horse sweat, and two of them had Mexican water canteens slung over their pommels. The man in front had long flaxen, greasy hair that hung from under a U.S. Army bill-cap. His face was as white as a carp's bely, Son thought, except for the sores that looked like a spray of bird shot in the dead skin. A withered scalp and what looked like a dried and blackened human ear hung from a beaded thong on his shirt.

"What can we do for you fellows?" Hugh said, grinning over his cigar, his walleye rolling with light.

"We was chasing a doe through the woods back there," the man in front said. "You seen her come out here?"

"No, sir, we didn't see no deer," Hugh said. "That's a pretty hard place to chase one, isn't it? Them brambles and tree limbs must have chewed you up."

"We been short on camp meat since we come down from the Red," the man said. "That norther's been pushing the game ahead of us each day."

"You can have what's left of our coffee and some jerky. We ain't got too much else," Hugh said.

"That's mighty kind," the man said. He and the other two riders dismounted and took turns drinking the scalding grinds out of the pot while they filled their hands with strips of jerked venison from the mule's pack.

"Where you fellows headed on the trace?" the man said.

"Maybe over to Bexar or on up to the plains. We ain't sure yet," Hugh said.

"What's it to you where we're headed, mister?" Son said.

"Nothing. I just figured if you all was riding to Bexar maybe we could head that way together. I heered the Mexicans was trying to conscript Americans into their army. I sure wouldn't want to be caught with just the three of us and run into a whole column of Mexicans that wanted to put us to soldiering again."

"Which army was you in?" Hugh said.

"Andy Jackson's, before they throwed us out."

"It looks to me like you taken some scalps of recent," Hugh said.

"We got jumped by Comanches up on the Red a couple of times. They get madder than hell when you shoot up their buffalo. I don't blame them, though. The herds is getting thinner and thinner. A fellow can do a whole sight better these days bringing back slaves from up north. One of my bunkies here made five hundred dollars in one month. He caught fourteen of them hiding in a cave."

"You fellows sure know how to turn a dollar, don't you?" Son said.

"You don't always get to choose the kind of living you make, mister," the man said.

"We're fixing to ride out, mister," Hugh said. "You can come along if you like, but we plan on camping early because my partner here has got a boil on his butt that don't let him ride too far in a day. We'll be behind you most of the way."

"We'll get together before dark," the man said.

The three men in deerskin got into their saddles and trotted their horses along the trace through the field of wind-blown grass. They posted on their thighs as though they had blisters from riding a long time.

"Why'd you let them off so easy?" Son said.

"I got them out in front of us, didn't I? You just have your rifle ready when they turn. Kill the other two, but leave scab-face alive. Sana, you keep way behind us, like your horse has gone lame, and you don't know what to do with it."

"You reckon they're going to hit us in an open field instead of in the woods?"

"Damn right, because scab-face there thinks he's a smartass, and he's going to do what he thinks we wouldn't figure him to. Oh Lord, the innocence of your children." Hugh clicked back the hammer on his revolver. "I sure hope this thing don't blow my head off. I got a feeling I'd do more damage with it if I gave it to them and let them shoot at me."

Five minutes later they watched the three riders slow their horses, then stop, as though they had forgotten something. The leader turned his horse around with a casual flick of the reins, and the other two men fanned out beside him. They rode slumped in the saddles with no weapons in sight.

"Yes, sir, they just remembered something they wanted to tell us," Hugh said. "You take the one on the left, and don't aim no higher than his nipples."

"Hugh, you might be wrong."

"I ain't. I been with too many of their kind. Scab-face is going to start grinning like a shit-eating cat, and then he'll move."

Son's hands were tight on his rifle stock. He began to worry about the powder they had gotten from Jack Tyler. It would be just like that sharper to mix black sand in it, he thought. Then the leader smiled and called out something at them in the wind. At the same time his hand went inside his coat and came out with a huge cap and ball pistol.

Son threw the rifle to his shoulder, raised in his stirrups, and sighted on the breastbone of the rider to the left of the leader. The pan flashed, and an almost simultaneous explosion roared in his ear and spooked his horse in a circle. He heard Hugh fire, then saw him cock the Colt with both hands and fire a second time. The man on the left had been blown backward off his horse and lay in the grass with one leg bent under him. The rider on the right was hit in the throat and was bent forward over his horse, roaring blood over its neck while he tried to pick the reins off the ground with one hand. The leader's pistol had misfired, and he sat frozen in the saddle, his face bloodless with fear and shock.

"Take him!" Hugh said.

Son kicked his boots into his horse's ribs and rode at a full gallop straight at the leader. The man tore the defective cap from his pistol and pushed another one into the firing hole. He raised the pistol just as Son swung the rifle by the barrel with both hands across his face. Son could feel the wood stock cut into the bone. The man's foot was twisted in the stirrup, and his horse dragged him thirty yards before it stopped and started tearing at the grass with its teeth.

The man with the wound in his throat was slumped motionless along his horse's neck, his open mouth a brilliant red.

"You done good, boy!" Hugh yelled. "I think you tore scab-face's head off his shoulders. Come over here and look at this one. Does that Kentucky do a job on a man. The ball went in as neat as a thumb hole and come out like a frying pan."

Son couldn't speak. He was shaking all over.

"Get out of it. It's over," Hugh said. Then, "Do you hear me? They're dead, except for scab-face, and he ain't far from it."

"What happened with your second shot?" Son's voice sounded far away from him.

"I just missed, that's all. I hit the first one so clean I figured I could catch scab-face in the side without even aiming. But ain't this some beautiful pistol? I had that sonofabitch cocked and ready to fire again two seconds after the first shot. If the Texians get a bunch of these they'll run Santa Anna plumb back to Mexico City."

"Ain't you got enough of that dead man?"

"I always admire good shooting, boy. And before you start to lecturing me again, you think about what they had in mind for us, not to say nothing about Sana."

"What'd you want to do with that other one?"

"That depends a whole lot on him."

They walked over to the unconscious man in the grass. Blood dripped from his nose into his unshaved face.

"Wake up, sweetheart," Hugh said, touching the man on the shoulder with his boot.

"He looks like his brains is busted loose," Son said.

"No, I think he's just turned into a possum. But we'll see." Hugh knelt beside the man and began pushing divots of grass into his mouth. The man gagged and spat and tossed his head sideways. His eyes rolled wildly.

"That's a little better, my friend," Hugh said. "Now, you listen to me real careful. We killed your bunkies and you're all on your own. So you're going to tell us why you was dogging us through them trees back there, and don't tell us you was running no deer."

"We seen you leave out of Tyler's this morning with all them supplies," the man said.

Hugh raised his fist high over his head and smashed it down into the man's face.

"Hold up, Hugh," Son said.

"My ass. The next one is going to have his brains running out his nose," Hugh said. "Why was you dogging us?"

"We rode into Tyler's about two hours before light. I seen you was drunk and you was trading off that string, and I figured we'd take you easy today."

Hugh hit him again, this time a short blow that brought the man's lips into his teeth.

"I reckon you just lie by habit, don't you?" he said. "There was a dozen men that left out of there this morning, most of them riding single with more money and supplies than we got. So I reckon we're going to get it out of you the Indian way. What do you think about that, Sana?"

"He tell," she said.

"We was going to kill you and take your supplies and animals, mister. The man your partner shot was after the squaw. What else you want out of me?"

"I can tell you're a toughie that don't get broke down easy," Hugh said. He slipped his bone-handle knife out of the buckskin scabbard on his side and began sharpening the edge with a flint over the man's face.

Then he pulled the man's flaxen hair back in his fist and placed the knife's edge between his ear and skull.

As Son stared at Hugh and the man lying on the ground, he didn't know which of their expressions looked more horrible. Involuntarily, he stepped forward to pull Hugh away, but Sana held his arm with both her hands.

"You only make worse," she said.

Hugh twisted the man's hair tighter in his fist and pressed the flat of the knife blade against his scalp.

"Last chance or say good-bye to it forever."

"Don't do it. Please," the man said. His mouth was trembling and tears ran out of his eyes. "A Frenchy named Landry has got two hundred dollars out on each of you."

"Where'd you see this Frenchy at?" Hugh said.

"In a saloon where the trace branches off toward San Felipe."

"What made you figure it was us he had the money out on?" Son said.

"He described that walleye. He said it looked like a black clam shell."

"You ain't off the point of my knife yet, asshole," Hugh said.

"There ain't anything else to tell you."

"Where's he supposed to pay you at?" Son said.

"Bexar or Matagorda Bay."

"So you was going to put us in a salt barrel and haul us around half of south Texas. You're lying again, boy," Hugh said.

The man was silent, his eyes reaching upward into the blue sky. Hugh hit him on the ear with the butt of the knife.

"He said to pickle your heads in a jar and leave the rest," the man said.

Hugh wiped the knife blade on the grass, slipped it in his scabbard, and got to his feet.

"This is the sonofabitch you thought I was being cruel on," he said to Son.

"What do we do about him?"

"Kill him," Sana said. Son turned and stared at her.

"She's right. He knows who we are and where we're at," Hugh said.

"Hugh, we got to stop it somewhere."

"He kill Indians' food and then show off Indian scalp."

"I got a feeling this boy would skin a skunk's bottom if it'd put some money in his pocket," Hugh said.

"I'm against it, and my say is half the vote here," Son said. Hugh looked down at the man on the ground.

"You see, me and my partner vote on everything," he said, "and he votes for your life. That's lucky for you, ain't it? The problem is that he don't have a ball in his rifle, and I still got three in this Colt. So that's unlucky for you."

"I ain't going to tell nobody," the man said.

"I know you ain't," Hugh said.

"Please, mister. I'm heading for Galveston, and you won't never see me again."

"Galveston is right down the pike from Matagorda Bay, ain't it?" Hugh said.

"I swear before Jesus I'll get out of Texas. You can kill me if you ever see me anywhere again."

Hugh took the revolver out of his belt and cocked the hammer back with his thumb. The man shook his head from side to side in the grass.

"Where'd you get that black ear you wear on your shirt?" Hugh said.

"I took it off a Comanche buck."

"You never fought an Indian buck in your life. Who'd you cut it off of?"

"A squaw that used to tote for us."

"Eat it."

"What?"

"You heered me," Hugh said, and placed the pistol barrel to the man's temple.

A few minutes later he had the man take off his boots and buckskin breeches. The man's white buttocks were puckered in the cold.

"I got a big bean fart working up in me right now," Hugh said. "I'll give you till it breaks loose to make them pine trees over yonder. Then I'm going to blow your skinny nuts all over this field."

They watched the man race through the grass toward the stand of pines, the unnatural whiteness of his legs flashing in the sun.

"I guess you was with the Harpe gang, wasn't you?" Son said.

"What you just seen is one way of doing it, boy. You either kill a man like that, or you shame him so he don't ever bother you again. He'll be afraid to sleep at night because of the dreams he'll have about us."

Behind them they heard the drone of deer flies in the grass.

"Let's get out of here," Hugh said.

"You reckon he was telling the truth about Landry being over in Bexar?"

"Shit, who knows? Landry might have lied to him, figuring scab-face would come out second best when he caught up with us and we'd cover him up in an ant pile. Piss on it, anyway. I need a drink. Sana, get that rum bottle out of my sack."

"Let's take their guns. We can sell them on down the trace."

"You're growing up all the time, ain't you?"

As they rode away with the looted guns and powder horns and flints, the wind blew out of the pines and pressed the green and yellow grass flat in the field, exposing the booted leg of a man twisted on his knee like a tilted cross.

CHAPTER

FIVE

They lived three weeks in the Tonkawa village on the west bank of the Brazos River. The river was dark green and full of fish, and the canebrakes along the banks were ten feet high and so thick that a rifle ball couldn't pass through them. Each evening the winter sky was lighted with sunsets of scarlet and turquoise and pink clouds, and in the morning the mist hung on the river and in the cane and the sun burned through it like a slow orange flame. The Tonkawas were a strange people who lived in conical thatched huts and married their in-laws, and neither Son nor Hugh could ever figure out their family relationships. The women covered their breasts with circles of yellow and black paint, and there was one large hut where they were forced to go during their menstrual cycle.

Sana found two of her uncles and three cousins in the village, and she spent most of her time with them, but each night she went with Son to gig bullfrogs by the light of a Mexican angle lamp along the river bank or string trot lines through the cattails. But he also knew she was gradually becoming one of her people again. On the third night he could tell she had painted her breasts, and she wore a coup feather tied to the end of her long black hair.

"I didn't think you was supposed to wear one of those unless you killed somebody," he said.

"I kill a Comanche when I was fourteen," she said. "He and two others try to take my mother."

Then sometimes in the stillness of cicadas she would squeeze his arm, kiss him on the neck and cheek, and whisper to him in her own language. She wore a string of blue morning glories on her shirt, and her black hair shone in the light from the angle lamp.

"What's that mean?" he said after the first time she did it.

"I not tell you."

"What kind of dumb game is that? I could say things you don't understand."

"What?" she said, smiling, her brown eyes moving over his face.

"A lot of things people say back in Tennessee."

"You such strange, nice boy. One day Indian teach you how to laugh. But you nice boy, anyway."

On a late wind-burned afternoon three Tonkawa hunters rode back into camp with their horses spent. The lead rider slipped off his horse without bothering to untie the bloodied and stiffened doe from the withers, and went directly into the chief's hut. A few minutes later the rider, the chief, and Sana found Son and Hugh fishing with throw lines on the edge of the canebrake.

"You all sounded like a buffalo coming through that cane," Hugh said.

"You leave, quick," Sana said.

"What is it?" Son said.

The chief and the hunter began to speak at once. The insides of the hunter's buckskin breeches were still wet with horse lather.

"He says many Mexicans and some strange Americans stop him earlier. He think they look for you," Sana said.

"Ask him about these Americans," Hugh said.

She spoke rapidly to the hunter, and he began to gesture in the air with his hands.

"He says they Americans who talk different and wear tall hats. They tell him they looking for two murderers. One is an old man with a big eye, and the other a tall boy with blond hair."

"Back in the shithouse again," Hugh said.

"How'd they get the Mexicans with them?" Son said.

"You remember that little horse raid we made with Iron Jacket? Them Mexicans ain't dumb. They know them and Landry want the same two skinned asses tacked up on a tree."

"Ask him how far away they are," Son said.

The hunter understood and pointed at the sun and motioned twice at the air with his cupped hand.

"He says they be here soon after the ducks fly down on the river," Sana said.

"Shit, that gives us till about a half hour after sunset. Let's pack it and haul ass," Hugh said.

"Where?"

"We go west, then head south behind them. This time we don't stop till we find Sam Houston's army. We could use a lot of company if Landry's got the Mexicans riding with him."

They walked back through the canebrake in the fading light, loaded their guns, saddled their horses, and stuffed one canvas bag from Tyler's full of smoked fish and venison. The sun had become a small crack of fire in the violet clouds on the horizon when they rolled their second change of clothes in their blankets and tied them on the backs of their saddles.

"You do what Hugh tell you. Stay with the Americans till those bad men go away," Sana said.

"I'll be back after we get finished soldiering. If this war comes out right, I'll have six hundred and forty acres of land, too," Son said.

"You not come back."

"I sure will."

"You change when you go away. You be like other Americans. It not bad."

"Hell, I'm not like other Americans. I'm a convict. I ain't got no more in common with the Americans you've knowed than them Frenchies that's chasing us."

"You want to set here and talk some more, or just invite the Mexicans to hang us up on their pig stickers?" Hugh said.

They rode in a gallop toward the low brown hills west of the village, and by the time they reached the first rise, great flocks of mallards and teal were winnowing across the sky and breaking formation to land on the river. The land was awash with the sun's red afterglow, and in the distance to the south they could make out two long black lines of riders.

"Stop it in them oaks over the top," Hugh called over his shoulder. "We better pour it on while we got the chance."

"I don't think they seen us in all this shadow, but they will for sure when we come off the other side." They made the top of the hill and rode into the trees. Hugh got down from his horse and tethered it to an oak limb. He squatted in the grass at the edge of the trees and stared back down the river at the column of riders.

"You got better eyes than me. Can you make out them men in front?" he said.

"No."

"They ain't army."

"I'm for hitting it, Hugh."

"Look behind you. There must be five miles of open country out yonder. Give it another ten minutes and we'll be gone into the dark like a couple of owls."

They watched the column turn into the village and the Tonkawas begin coming out of the circle of huts. The last of the twilight's shadows seemed to gather into the earth, and the wind blew off the river and rattled through the canebrake.

"Somebody's starting a fire down there," Son said.

"They're probably going to pass some whiskey around till somebody gets drunk enough to tell them where we're at. There's always two or three that'll skin out a bunkie when their grog starts to run short."

They saw a small flame glow on the ground in the middle of the village, then the fire leaped higher in the wind and silhouetted the two men throwing dried brush into it. The flames cracked upward in a spray of yellow sparks and burned away the shadows back to the ring of huts.

"Look in front of the fire. It's him," Son said.

"It sure is. Or one just like him. No other man in Texas would wear pantaloons and a tall hat like that."

"I don't know why, but I feel funny looking at him."

"He ain't exactly the person you was most wanting to see."

"No. It's different. I don't know how to say it. It's almost like I feel scared."

"You're seeing yourself back in prison again. Forget it. We ain't never going back there."

"You was right about the whiskey. That mule must have four or five kegs slung on it."

"In a half hour that camp is going to be like a crazy house. Out on the plains I seen them trade off everything they owned to keep the spigot open."

"You reckon they'll find out about Sana?"

"I doubt it. Even a drunk Indian knows what'll happen to him if he turns against his own kind."

"What?"

"They drive them out of the tribe. It's like they don't exist no more. It's the worst thing that can happen to them. Come on, let's lead our mounts down the other side of the hill and then cut southwest toward the Colorado. Sam Houston's over in that country somewheres."

Son continued to stare down the incline. Hugh pushed him in the rump with his boot.

"Let's get moving. Stop worrying about her. She's a smart girl. She ain't going to get herself caught."

"We should have taken her with us."

"Sometimes you can't do everything right, boy. She understands that. You ought to learn it, too. But if you really want to, you can send a ball down there in the middle of them. Then they'll blow us into chicken guts and you won't have these problems no more."

"All right, let's get out of here. You think they can cut our trail in the dark?"

"Maybe. But once we get to the hill country they ain't going to have no trail to follow. The best tracker I ever knowed couldn't follow deer sign through them rocks and hollows. Some of them stretches down by the Colorado ain't got enough dirt for a lizard to dig a hole and fart in."

They led their horses off the back side of the hill in the dark, and when they reached the tall buffalo grass in the field they mounted and rode toward the evening star that lay like a cold diamond on the horizon.

At sunrise they came out of a woods onto a large farm with rick fences bordering the fields and a smooth road that led back to a rambling house set among chinaberry and live oak trees. The blacks were already at work in the fields, clearing stumps with mules and burning them in huge trash fires. The house was painted white and had a breezeway through the center and a verandah that ran all the way around the building. In back were the barns and a dozen split-log slave cabins placed so neatly in a row that an arrow could fly the entire length of the front porches without touching a post. The blacks and mules moved about in the mist and the smoke of the trash fires like silent half-formed creatures.

"I bet we're going to meet a white man that gets the most out of his darkies," Hugh said.

Son felt a strange sense of discomfort when they rode their horses at a walk down the lane toward the house. It was the same feeling he'd had when he'd entered a public house for the first time in New Orleans and had been told by a slave to go around to the side door.

"I reckon that's the overseer," Hugh said. "Them kind sure look all alike, don't they? One step above the niggers and about five down from any other white man."

The overseer was a sallow man on horseback in a straw hat and wool coat with his trousers tucked inside his muddy boots. He rested a cup of coffee on the pommel of his saddle.

"Hello!" Hugh called.

The man nodded without replying.

"We need some directions and some breakfast if you got it," Hugh said.

"We got food in the poke," Son whispered.

"We ain't got coffee and eggs and fatside."

"Where you wanting to go?" the overseer said, his face a mixture of distrust and dislike.

"Well, that's the problem. We ain't quite sure," Hugh said. "Can you give us breakfast? We got the money to pay for it."

"You don't pay no money on Mr. Reilly's place. Ride your horses around by the back porch."

"We thank you," Hugh said.

"Tell him to stick his back porch up his butt hole," Son said.

"What do you expect?" Hugh said. "You want a uniformed nigger to serve us on silver plate out on the verandah? Besides, the smokehouse is in back."

They walked their horses through the live oaks and chinaberry trees around the side of the house. Wooden flower boxes were nailed below the shuttered windows. A terraced rose garden shored up with large rocks sloped down to a creek that was lined with willow trees and wild fern. Directly behind the back verandah was a log smoke-house, and they could smell the sides of salted pork dripping into the ash. A moment later a black man wearing a brushed coat and trousers and a shirt with a collar came out on the verandah and set a fire-blackened coffee pot and two cups on the table.

"You gentlemens set down. I'll bring your breakfast directly, and Mr. Reilly will give you your directions," he said, and disappeared through the door again.

"You ever seen a darky like that outside of New Orleans?" Son said.

"They got them like that in Natchez. They even teach them how to read and write so they can do the marketing."

"There's something about this place that just don't hit my nose right."

"You're still remembering what them French gentlemen done to you in the courtroom," Hugh said.

"That ain't it. Figure it this way. Ever since we come across the Sabine we ain't seen nobody with money like this. Any farms we run across was about forty acres of scrub land with one plow mule on it. How do you reckon this Reilly fellow keeps a hold of a place like this?"

"That is something to study on."

"You damn right it is."

The black man came through the door with a tray of grits, fried fatback, and scrambled eggs between his hands. Before the door could swing shut on the counter weight, he caught it with his shoulder for his owner to walk through. The white man was tall with an angular face and a beard that was squared below the jaw. He wore a shawl under his housecoat, and a large ring of keys hung from his belt. He looked as though he had been caught between undressing from the night and preparing for his day as proprietor of something very large and solid and his.

"How can I be of service to you gentlemen?" he said.

They were both surprised at his Irish accent.

"We was riding all night and didn't feel like another cold breakfast and thought we might take advantage of your kindness," Hugh said. "Besides, the trace petered out in them woods back there, and we got a little bit lost."

"My overseer said you weren't quite sure where you were going."

"We're headed down toward the Colorado and maybe over to the Guadalupe eventually," Hugh said, and tore at a piece of fatback with his teeth.

"You won't have any trouble, then. You'll catch the trace again just west of my property, and you just stay in a southwesterly direction."

"I figured it was kind of a dumb question to ask," Hugh said. "But you can't ever tell what's waiting for you down the pike these days."

"How's that?" Mr. Reilly said.

"With the Mexicans and the Texians shooting at each other and a lot of crazy men waiting to rob you at every turn in the woods," Hugh said.

"You seem well-armed enough to take care of yourself. Is that the Colt's revolver I've been hearing about?"

"Yes, sir, it is. I can get off five balls with it and draw blood faster than a chicken getting pecked to death. Jack Tyler over by the Trinity give it to me. You ever heered of him?"

"I'm afraid I don't know him," Mr. Reilly said. "If you think you know your way now, I'll be about my chores."

"We was looking for somebody in particular down on the Colorado," Hugh said.

"Hugh," Son said.

"I wondered if you might know where Sam Houston is at these days," Hugh said. His walleye was lighted with delight.

"Why would you want to find Sam Houston?"

"We're fixing to join up with him."

"You're insurrectionists, are you?"

"From what I hear it ain't no insurrection," Hugh said. "The Mexicans been throwing Texians into jails for fifteen years. Back in Kentucky we wouldn't have put up with that shit for more time than it takes to load a rifle. We'd fry Santa Anna in his own grease."

"Leave as soon as you finish your breakfast."

"I never knowed no Irishman to side with a tyrant, mister," Hugh said. "You must be a different breed from the ones I fought alongside with at Chalmette."

"You finish and get out."

Hugh chewed a large piece of fatback in his mouth and spit it into his plate.

"We done finished, mister," he said. "And before you walk away sniffing at the air like there's a bad smell in it, think about what it's going to be like if Sam Houston and Jim Bowie win this thing. My point is a fellow in a pretty shawl and dress like that ought not to be flinging his slop jar into the wind."

They rode laughing down the front road between the sunlit fields, the wind in their faces, while the overseer and the slaves pulling stumps stared after them curiously.

They wandered for weeks through the hill country of south central Texas, across the Colorado and the Guadalupe and over toward San Antonio de Bexar, then south on the Guadalupe again. The rolling hills and steep cliffs were the largest Son had seen since he left Tennessee. The pebble-bottomed streams were a clear green, and the banks were covered with cottonwoods and willows. Sometimes when they rode along a natural fault where they could see miles of the country at once, his head would swim with the enormous breadth and diversity of the horizon. The rocky ground was dotted with live oaks and blackjack and mesquite trees, and there were chains of lakes that sloped away toward another wide green river that cut its way through canyon walls that a ground squirrel couldn't climb.

Once they got within twenty miles of Bexar and were told that Ben Milam's men had taken the town for the Texians, although a ball had been driven through Milam's brain on the third day of the battle. They almost decided to ride into the town because Hugh thought James Bowie was there, but they still had a terrible question mark left from the slave hunter's story about Emile Landry's promise to pay a reward in Bexar.

They found Sam Houston and his army outside of Gonzales on the Guadalupe River. It was mid-morning and raining hard, and they saw the tents and lean-to shelters spread through a piney woods. The rain was sluicing off their hat brims and driving into their faces as they tried to focus through the gray light on the woods and estimate the number of men camped there.

"It sure don't look like a lot," Hugh said.

"You reckon that's just part of it?" Son said.

"I hope so, because I wouldn't want to be here if Santa Anna come marching with a thousand or so Mexicans up the pike."

"Stand and say who you are, mister," a picket called out from the edge of the trees.

"They sure don't put their pickets out too far," Hugh said.

"You better sing the right song, mister, or I'm going to put a ball through your eye," the picket yelled.

"Who the hell do we look like, the king and queen of England?" Hugh shouted.

There was no response from the woods, and in the waving sheets of rain they still couldn't make out where the voice had come from. Son stood forward in his stirrups and cupped his hands over his mouth.

"We want to join up with you. We got our own guns and grub," he said.

"Ride in," the picket replied.

"They're a choicy bunch of sonsofbitches, ain't they?" Hugh said.

"Take it easy today, Hugh. Don't see how many people you can get mad at us our first day in the army."

"They're damn glad to have us, boy, and don't forget it. I bet there ain't hardly any of these men that knows anything about soldiering. I learned more against the redcoats at Chalmette than this bunch could put together between them."

They rode into the shelter of the trees and saw the picket walk out from behind a short earthen works shored up with sawed pine logs. He wore deerskin clothes, Indian moccasins, and a flop hat, and carried a Kentucky rifle in his hands. His eyes were like agate as he looked at them.

"Where you come from?" he said.

"We been up on the Brazos with the Indians a bit, and then we wandered all over the hill country looking for you all," Hugh said. "I never seen an army that could lose itself so well."

"I don't mean that. Where you come from?" the picket asked.

"Kentucky and Tennessee," Son said. "What the hell difference does it make?"

"You seen any Mexicans?"

"Just get your thumb off the hammer a minute and we'll tell you," Hugh said.

"We ain't seen none since we left the Brazos," Son said.

"You see that wide tent yonder?" the picket said. "Take your horses over there and don't get down till I tell you."

"We went to a lot of trouble to find you, and we ain't in the mood for playing no games out in a wet woods," Hugh said.

"General Houston don't let nobody sign up till he talks with them first," the picket said.

They walked their horses over the thick layer of pine needles on the forest floor. Dripping tree limbs swung back against their faces, and unshaved soldiers in buckskin and homespun clothes looked out at them from the gloom of their tents and lean-tos. The smoke from the few camp fires flattened in the drizzle through the trees and hung low on the ground. The picket walked to the flap of the wide tent that was hung on two ropes crisscrossed between four pine trunks.

"General, this is Corporal Burnett. There's two fellows out here that say they're from Tennessee and Kentucky and want to join up."

"Send them in, please."

"Yes, sir." The picket untied the leather thong from the tent pole and pulled back the flap, then looked up into the rain. "You all go in."

Son and Hugh got down from their horses and stepped inside the warmth and dryness of the tent. Sam Houston sat behind a table made from a half dozen board planks nailed across the tops of two pine stumps. His hair was grown down on his shoulders and hung in curls on his brow; because of his narrow shoulders and the lack of color in his thin lips he looked almost effeminate to Son at first glance, until Son looked again at the wide forehead and the deep-set eyes that were either hazel or gray (he couldn't tell which) and stared at him as steadily as a cocked musket. He wore a navy coat with large buttons on each side of the front, and a blanket was draped around the back of his chair. A pewter container of ink with a stained quill in it was set on top of an unfinished letter in front of him. In the moment's hush after the picket had fastened the flap behind him, Son felt not only his own but also Hugh's sudden lack of preparation in front of this very different man.

"I understand you gentlemen want to join the army," Houston said. The voice was Tennessee, from the mountains, with the soft and deceptive inflection of the Cumberland men whom Son and Hugh had known all their lives.

"Yes, sir, General," Hugh said. "We been hunting you all over God's green earth. We done give up when somebody told us you was right outside Gonzales."

"Why do you want to join the army?" The eyes never blinked with the question, as though it were something very natural to ask with the rain ticking on the canvas roof like a bad watch running out of time.

"The way things are now, you either got to get in the army or have the Mexicans shooting at you half the time, anyway," Hugh said.

Son looked directly at the general's eyes and saw that the words never touched inside. "We heered you was giving six hundred and forty acres to any soldier that would stick it out to the end," he said.

"You can get more than that from the Mexicans just by signing an oath of allegiance to Mexico City," Houston said.

"We wouldn't do nothing like that," Hugh said. "I fought under Andy Jackson at New Orleans, just like you done at Horseshoe Bend. We wouldn't never support no tyrant like Santa Anna."

"I see you have one of Sam Colt's revolvers. How do you like it?" The voice was disarming, a relaxation like a flame being taken away from wax.

"It's a hell of a pistol, General. When I traded for it over at Jack Tyler's I thought I'd be safer in front of it than behind it because everything Jack trades is junk. His beer is so bad you just as lief pour it on the ground without bothering to run it through your pipes." Hugh's words were coming too fast, and there was a fine wire of strain in his voice. Son couldn't believe it. "Then my partner and me got jumped by three slave hunters this side of the Trinity, and I snapped off two shots at them fellows before they—"

"One of my officers, Sam Walker, has a Colt. I wish I had a few more of them. Why did these slave hunters jump you?"

Hugh looked blankly back at him and fingered the damp edge of his coat.

"They was fixing to rob us," he said.

"It's strange that three slave hunters would attack two armed white men when they could make more profit and have less trouble with runaway Negroes."

"General, them men was after us because we're escaped convicts from Louisiana," Son said. "We killed a guard over there, and his brother has got two hundred dollars on each of our heads. He's been running us all over Texas, and he liked to got us a few weeks back on the Brazos. He had a bunch of Mexicans with him, too, because we raided a Mexican horse pen with the Indians just after we come across the Sabine."

"Did you have to kill that guard?"

"I can't answer that one too good to myself," Son said.

"How well do you shoot that Kentucky?" Houston asked.

"As good as the next man. We ain't gone hungry for camp meat with it."

"What else have you done with it?"

"Sir?"

"You didn't kill that guard in Louisiana with it. Can you kill a Mexican with it?"

"I dropped one of them slave hunters, General."

Houston picked up a carpet bag from under the table and took out two printed enlistment forms. They were worded in the grandiloquent language of a man who had memorized hundreds of passages from the *Iliad* and *Odysseey* while living among the Cherokees:

TEXAS FOREVER

We pledge to rally to the standard against the usurper of the South and all those who deny the rights of freeborn men. With valor and our faith in God we will not desist until the violators of our homes and farms are driven forever from the soil of the Republic. The justice of our cause will be evidenced by the gallantry and spirit with which we serve it. Our birthright and country will be maintained, or we will perish in defense of it.

_____

His signature or mark

Hugh made his mark on the line, and Son labored carefully with the quill until he had drawn his full name.

"When do we start kicking some Mexican butt, General?" Hugh said.

"That depends on many things, gentlemen. But now you should

go back with Corporal Burnett and build a lean-to for yourselves,"
he said.

"Sir, one other thing. Do you know where Jim Bowie is at?"
Hugh said.

"He's in Bexar. Do you know him?"

"Hell, yes. We drunk and played cards together many a time in
New Orleans."

"What did you think of him?"

"He's meaner than piss boiling in a pot when he's mad. I seen
him tear up a public house once after somebody stole his purse.
He run eight men through a window before he found the one that
done it."

Houston laughed out loud.

"That sounds very much like Jim in his cups," Houston said. "I'm
very glad to have you gentlemen on our side."

He said it with genuine warmth, and both Hugh and Son pulled
back their shoulders just a little.

For the next two months their life in the army involved almost
everything in a soldier's experience except fighting a war. They
sawed firewood and hauled water, built earthen works, dug latrines
and filled them in again. Each morning after muster they marched
four hours back and forth in the open field next to the woods and
practiced firing in staggered volley lines, snapping their hammers
on empty flash pans and cap holes and aiming at a distant grove
of live oaks. The ennui became contagious among them. Half the
time they were not listening when their noncommissioned officers
shouted drill instructions at them, and they stepped on each other's
heels and collided into the man in front when someone didn't hear
the order to halt. The idea of taking orders from men like themselves
was a contradiction in their minds, a violation of the politics that
brought them into the army in the first place: to rid their community
of a tyrannical authority that made their lives wretched.

Also, the noncommissioned officers had little if any more experience in the army than the enlisted men. Often they argued among
themselves in front of their men and sometimes devised training
plans that turned into a carnival at their own expense, such as the
time that Corporal Burnett sent forty men on a wide circle through

a woods and forgot to tell them what to do when they got there. When he found them that afternoon half of them were drunk and sick on green tequila they had bought off a traveling Mexican liquor supplier.

Of the enlisted men who talked back to the noncommissioned officers and complained incessantly, Hugh was the worst. He yawned loudly and belched during muster, drove the wood wagon over a corporal's foot, shot at a deer when he was standing picket and aroused the whole camp, got drunk whenever he could buy tequila, broke wind deliberately while at attention, and always offered advice about a better way to do something. One morning during drill Corporal Burnett had them form into a defensive square in the middle of the field and kneel in a firing position.

"All right, this is what is called the 'British square,'" he said. "You use it when you get caught out in the open and you ain't got no cover. As long as you hold the square nobody can fire on your back or your flank."

"It's real good for keeping everybody in one place so a cannon ball can wipe out half of them, too," Hugh said.

"What?"

"When we pushed the redcoats back to the Gulf at Chalmette, they went into squares all over the field. Our eight-pounders blowed guts and brains into the tops of the trees. I think they done the same thing in the Revolution, too."

"You start tonight on another latrine, Allison."

"I'm just telling you and these other boys what that square's worth. You try to fight the Mexicans anywhere in the open and they'll shove that musket up your butt sideways. General Sam knows that. Why the hell you think we cut bait anytime there's Mexicans a day's ride away? This war ain't going to get won fighting like no redcoats."

The corporal was furious, but he couldn't argue with Hugh's experience, and he also knew that the general had no plans to engage the enemy in any kind of open, or worse, enclave situation.

"Fall out, Allison, and get started on that latrine now," he said. "When I get back to camp I'm going to see if I can't do something permanent about you."

"Like what?" Hugh said, taking a twist of tobacco from his pocket.

"Like getting your ass out of this army."

"I'll be here when we pop our first caps on them Mexicans. When that time comes, you just stay behind me and find out how it's done." He balanced his rifle on his shoulder, holding the barrel in the crook of his arm, and walked back toward the woods to begin digging another latrine.

One morning Erastus Deaf Smith needed three men to go with him to Bexar and deliver a message to James Bowie and pick up a wagon load of powder, caps, flints, and lead bars for shot. Smith was Houston's scout, without rank or title except "scout," and he looked as though he had been hammered together out of pig iron. Any movement of his thick body made the muscles tighten against his buckskin clothes, and his broad face and wide-set eyes had the resolution of a skillet. A fever had destroyed most of his hearing when he was a child, and he talked in a quacking voice as he tried to imitate what he thought words should sound like. But he read lips, in both English and Spanish, he could see a deer flash through a dappled woods a half mile away, and sometimes he would suddenly rein his horse to a stop, dismount and stand silently for a moment, then point in the direction of approaching riders just before they came into sight. He was absolutely without fear and the only man in the Texas army whom Houston trusted completely.

Every soldier within earshot of his quacking voice volunteered for the trip to Bexar. Corporal Burnett appointed himself as an accepted volunteer, then Hugh pushed through the others and stood directly in front of Smith so his lips could be read.

"That's me and Son Holland, Deaf," he said. "I know Jim Bowie. He ain't going to be able to read General Sam's letter unless I get him sober first. I ain't sure that drunk sonofabitch can read, anyway. I'll probably have to do it for him."

"Hold it," Corporal Burnett said.

"Deaf don't take no orders from you. Ain't that right, Deaf? The general told you to pick out some good men, and you got them right here."

"You can't drink with Bowie in Bexar," Smith said.

"You ever seen me drunk?" Hugh said. "I ain't like these others. I wouldn't touch that green Mexican piss they drink."

"You're supposed to be cutting wood today, Allison," Corporal Burnett said.

"I done that last night while you was sleeping on picket. How about it, Deaf? I really want to see Jim again."

"Take two powder horns each," Smith said. "Tell the cook to give you beef in your ration and none of that salted pork. Get gum coats from somebody if you ain't got them. It's going to be stringing frogs by this afternoon."

The sky was blue with only a few pink clouds on the horizon.

"If that's what you say, Deaf. We ain't going to be but a minute."

Hugh crawled inside his and Son's lean-to, stuck the Colt's revolver inside his belt, handed Son his rifle, and stooped back into the light with his short-barrel musket in one hand and his sailcloth sack with the sewed tie string in the other. They started walking toward the cooking area in the center of the woods. Hugh's walleye was as bright as a black marble. "You ain't thinking right, Hugh," Son said. "Maybe Landry or some of them other Frenchies are still there."

"I don't give a shit if they are. I can't take no more of this hiding in a rat hole."

"You was talking about not being foolish, and now you're ready to put our balls on a stump just to get away from camp for a few days."

"Ben Milam took that town for the Texians. We're in the Texian Army, ain't we? And Jim Bowie's there. He'd hack that mulatto's head off if they tried to put manacles on us."

"You ain't thinking about the two-hundred-dollar bounty that Landry probably promised every piece of white trash in Bexar, either," Son said.

"They'll have to take on Jim, too, if they're going to get it. And there ain't no white man that stupid."

"Hugh, you just ain't using your head like you usually do. Maybe if we don't do nothing dumb now, we'll be out of all that trouble back in Louisiana."

"You make your own selections. I'm going to see Jim, I'm going to get drunk with him, and I'm going to forget all them latrines I dug because a corporal with pap still on his mouth told me to do it."

"That ain't what you told Deaf."

"You don't ever learn nothing, do you? Deaf wants you and me because we got these leg-iron scars on our ankles. We ain't going to desert and ride down the pike to find a better deal with a dumb ass like James Fannin, and we ain't going to shoot off our mouth to no Mexican spy in a saloon or jenny-barn. He wouldn't take nobody with him unless they was the best, and I got a feeling that General Sam already told him me and you was going."

They stood by the large Dutch oven built of field stones, where the cooks were frying salted pork and boiling a gruel made of cracked corn and molasses in an iron pot. The cooks were a filthy lot, their faces and beards blackened by soot, and Son had heard that two of them had the clap.

Hugh handed one of them his sailcloth sack.

"We're going out with Deaf this morning. He says to fill it up with beef and any pickled tomatoes and melon you got."

"You want what?" the cook said, staring back with his grimy face above the smoke.

"Deaf don't want no salted pork. That's clear enough, ain't it? Just give us some of that smoked beef and any pickled tomatoes or melon that you ain't ate yourself."

"Allison, you lying sonofabitch, you tried this on me before. You get out of my kitchen or I'll give you another eye that looks like that ugly one you already got." The cook had a long pine branch in his hand that he had been using to stoke the fire.

"Maybe you better go back and talk with Deaf about it, cook," Son said. "There he is over by General Sam's tent. Lookie there, Sam's coming out the flap now."

"I wish somebody would tell me what the hell is going on around here," the cook said, opening the tie string on Hugh's sack. "I have to feed all you miserable sonsofbitches, and you don't give me nothing in turn except trouble and some half-ass story about you got to go off with Deaf. Nobody told me a damn thing about it. If you can't shit in the morning, you blame it on me. If it runs down your leg, you blame it on me, too. Now Deaf sends you in here for what little preserves I got left to keep you all from getting scurvy, and somebody's going to be bitching about that, too. You take this, Allison, and tell that stupid sonofabitch Deaf to learn how to use the human language so this camp don't turn into one big latrine."

It started raining hard that afternoon, and they were still five miles from Bexar when they stopped late the next night and slept in a farmer's barn. The following morning they rode into town, and the sand-colored stucco buildings with their Spanish ironwork and the cobblestone streets were wet and brilliant in the sunlight. The town reminded Son of New Orleans, except it was filled with Texas soldiers who seemed as out of place there as an occupying army in a foreign country. The saloons were crowded early in the day with men who spoke in Kentucky, Tennessee, and Georgia accents, and they behaved as though it were July Fourth back in the United States. When Son thought of the despondency in his camp on the Guadalupe, he wondered if these men were fighting in the same war as Houston's soldiers. He reached over and touched Deaf on the shoulder.

"These bastards act like they popped their last cap on the Mexicans," he said.

Deaf stretched his arms on the pommel of his saddle and shook his head.

"I said they act like there ain't no war," Son said.

"He understood you," Hugh said.

"Look at them two in front of the eating house. They're so drunk they can't stand up," Son said.

"What do you want to do, Deaf?" Hugh said.

"You all eat, and I'll find Bowie."

"I'll go with you."

"No, you won't," Deaf said.

"Hell, Deaf, that's my old friend."

"You'll see him later. He's got to write an answer to Sam first."

"All right, damn it, but you tell him Hugh Allison's in Bexar and he better have his dirty bum sober when I see him."

Son, Hugh, and the corporal tied their horses to an iron tethering post in front of the eating house while Deaf rode down the cobbled street toward the other end of town.

"How's he know where he's going?" Son said.

"There's probably a card parlor down yonder where Jim's lightening everybody's pockets."

"Deaf better not find him there," Corporal Burnett said.

"Your ass, Burnett. Jim Bowie don't make changes in what he does for no man."

"He sure as hell will when the general finds out what he's let this army turn into," the corporal said.

Inside the stucco building, most of the tables were filled with men in buckskin clothes, and Mexican women carried out trays of frijoles, huevos rancheros, tortillas, and steaks from a huge open kitchen in the back. The air was heavy with tobacco smoke, and some of the tables had bottles of rum and tequila on them.

"That food smells like it come out of a pepper patch," Son said.

"That ain't nothing to what it'll feel like when it comes out later," Hugh said. "But we're going to have a little drink of that Mexican gargle water to smooth it out a bit."

"I'll be damned if you are," the corporal said.

"Burnett, back at camp you can tell me to dig shit holes all you want," Hugh said. "But we're in Bexar now, and you ain't nothing but a wagon escort under Deaf just like we are. Hey, you boys move over and let some of Sam Houston's best set down."

They rolled eggs with chili peppers and strips of steak inside tortillas and ate them in huge mouthfuls. The peppers made Son's eyes water and his stomach burn, but the food was so good he hardly chewed before he swallowed again. Then they each ate a bowl of frijoles with more tortillas and divided a pot of coffee among the three of them. They listened to the conversation around them, and it was a strange one to hear after their experience in the camp on the Guadalupe. The soldiers at the tables talked of Ben Milam tearing General Cos's army to pieces when he took the town in December, of James Fannin marching any day on Matamoros, of pursuing Santa Anna deep into Mexico and hanging him by his thumbs from a mesquite tree. Their breaths were sour with alcohol and refried beans, and Son noticed that half of them had left their weapons somewhere else.

Hugh reached across the table and picked up a bottle of rum that another man had been drinking from.

"You don't mind if I buy a drink out of your bottle, do you?" he said.

"Go right ahead, Sam Houston's best," the man said. There were only three teeth in the front of his head, and they hung there like twisted pieces of bone.

"From the way you fellows talk, there ain't much left to this war except getting paid for it," Hugh said.

"That depends on how you figure it," the man said. "There might be some more ass-kicking done down south of us."

"I'd sure like to get in on that. Just where are you going to start kicking these asses?" Hugh said.

"Anywhere we catch them at," the man said.

"I heered Santa Anna might have five or six thousand men down on the Rio Grande somewhere. Is that the people that gets their butts stuck in the fire?" Hugh said.

"What are you trying to say, mister?" another man said.

"Nothing. We been camped over by Gonzales so long we don't know what's going on with the rest of the army. Was you boys with Ben Milam when he took Bexar?"

"You damn right we were."

"I bet it was a tough fight, wasn't it?" Hugh said.

"You're drinking my liquor and trying my patience at the same time, mister. You want to get to your point or just walk out of here?"

"Let's find Deaf," the corporal said.

"We got time for that," Hugh said. "I just want to know if there's any truth to the story that most of General Cos's troops was a bunch of raggedy-ass convicts. I heered some of them shot theirself in the foot so they wouldn't have to fight."

"That's a lie."

"It's just a story a fellow told us over in Gonzales."

"It's a damn lie, and you take it back."

"Like hell I will," Hugh said, his voice level and mean.

"We're leaving, mister. You own the place," Son said. "We don't give a shit if you fought convicts or every Mexican from here to Mexico City. But you touch that dirk and I'll put a hole in your face as big as your plate."

Outside, the wind blowing off the San Antonio River was cold against their faces. Clouds were moving over the hills south of town, and large areas of sunlight and shadow swept across the waving grass.

"You done all right in there," Hugh said.

"You two should be locked up in a crazy house," Corporal Burnett said.

"We didn't deal that play. Them fellows did with their big mouths," Hugh said.

"Allison, you got something inside you that don't let you leave trouble alone, and one of these days it's going to put you in a box." The corporal untethered his horse angrily and pushed hard in the stirrup when he swung up in the saddle.

"Lots have tried it, but the likes of them in there sure ain't going to do it," Hugh said.

"Forget it," Son said.

"I tell you, this is a hell of an army to have to fight a war with," the corporal said, looking straight ahead as they rode toward the other end of town.

"Ain't that Deaf's horse tied up the other side of that paint?" Son said.

"And I bet that big roan with the Mexican saddle is Jim's. He always did ride fancy," Hugh said.

Bowie's headquarters were in a brown adobe building with evenly spaced cedar logs jutting out of the mud bricks along the roof. During the siege of the town in December the Mexicans had torn out one window to ground level and put a cannon in it to command the street, and the area around the sand-bagged hole was pocked from rifle fire. In the front room there was a plank bar with bottles of tequila and corn whiskey and bowls of chili peppers on it, and dirty hand towels hung from nails driven into the plank. Dark men who looked like Acadians out of the Louisiana marshes were drinking at the bar, and each of them wore a large knife in a scabbard and had his rifle leaned at his elbow.

"Mean-looking sonsofbitches, ain't they?" Hugh said when they walked in.

To one side of the bar was a thick oak door that was partly opened, and behind it they could hear Deaf's quacking voice.

"Is Jim Bowie in there?" Hugh said.

The dark men stared at him without replying.

"I said is Jim Bowie in there?"

They still didn't answer, and Hugh started toward the door. One of the dark men stepped in front of him and wagged his finger in Hugh's face and shook his head.

"What's the matter, you dumb or something?" Hugh said.

The man said something in French.

"Talk United States," Hugh said.

"Take it easy. We'll just wait on Deaf," Son said.

"I hoped I wouldn't have to see another Frenchman after I left Louisiana, and I come all the way to Bexar to meet an asshole like this."

Son and Corporal Burnett looked quickly at the man to see if he had understood. The man's dark eyes continued to stare at Hugh with the same resolute expression.

"Hell, let's get a drink. I'll buy it," Hugh said.

"Deaf don't—" the corporal began.

"Deaf don't care," Hugh said. "He's got other things on his mind. Listen to him carrying on in there."

Son listened to Deaf's strange voice and realized that this was the first time he had ever heard him speak angrily to anyone. The quacking sound rose and fell, and many of the words were unintelligible, but there was no doubt that Deaf was becoming furious about something.

The Mexican bartender poured clear whiskey into three shot glasses, and they sipped it neat and chased it with salted chili peppers. The whiskey had been aged in a burned-out barrel, and the charcoal taste hung in the glass like smoke. Even the corporal was enjoying it and didn't object when Son ordered another round.

"That's the first time I ever heered anybody raise hell with Jim like that and get away with it," Hugh said.

"Deaf ain't one to worry about whether somebody likes what he says," the corporal said

"I got to grant you that," Hugh said. "He ain't afraid of too much. But he sounds like he wants to tear Jim's balls out. Maybe I ought to go in there and straighten it out."

"Maybe you ought to finish your drink," Son said.

Deaf came out of the room, his sun-tanned face bright with anger, and let the oak door swing back against its iron hinges. He went to the bar and held up two fingers at the bartender, who poured a double shot into the glass. Through the open door they could see a man in pantaloons and a short brown jacket with Mexican buttons seated behind a table. He coughed violently into a handkerchief, then wiped his mouth and grinned at Hugh.

"I knew they couldn't keep Hugh Allison in any Frenchman's jail," he said.

"How you doing, Jim? Lord, it's good to see you."

"Come on in." He held up a cup with his fingers. "And bring something for this."

Hugh's face was shining with pride as he picked up a bottle of whiskey from the bar and went inside the room.

"Close it so we can do ourselves some serious drinking," the man said.

Son turned to Deaf, whose jawbone was working like a damaged nerve against his cheek.

"He don't look too healthy. What was going on in there, anyway?" Son said.

"He's going to fortify the mission."

Son looked at him, not understanding.

"Sam thinks he ought to blow it up and move out of Bexar," Deaf said.

"Move where?" the corporal said.

"East, with us. What do you think will happen if they get caught inside them walls?" Deaf said.

Neither the corporal nor Son knew how to answer.

"I ought not to get mad at him. Sam left the choice up to him," Deaf said. "But a beaver don't go into a hole unless he's got a back door."

"Why don't he want to pull out?" Son said.

"He figures if they don't stop Santa Anna here, the Mexicans will sweep through east Texas. I'm going out in the hills south of town. Make sure Allison is sober when I get back tonight."

"That ain't easy to do," the corporal said.

"He damn well better be." Deaf set his glass on the bar and walked out the door. In the square of yellow light, they saw him jerk back the reins on his horse, wheel it in a circle, and bring his moccasins hard into its ribs.

"I think Deaf just told us something," the corporal said.

"Don't worry about Hugh. He sobers up fast," Son said.

"If you can get the bottle out of his hand first."

"Get him out of there, then."

"I ain't going in there."

"Then quit worrying. I ain't seen the situation yet that Hugh don't handle."

* * *

But five hours later Son was not as confident. The corporal had ridden across the river to look at the mission and Son was eating a bowl of frijoles in the eating house when Hugh found him. Hugh was drunk in a way that Son hadn't seen him before. He looked as though he had been drinking for two days rather than a few hours. His face was bloodless and the whites of his eyes had turned yellow.

"You and Bowie must have licked the cup dry," Son said.

"No, he went to sleep about three hours ago."

"Where you been?"

"I found a jenny-barn down by the river."

"Eat some food."

"I don't want none. Them beans turns your skin brown, anyway."

"You ought to eat something."

"I'm going to have another drink."

"Deaf rode out in the hills. He's coming back tonight and we're leaving."

"I'll be ready."

"You're really in your cup, Hugh."

"Jim's awful sick. I think it's the pneumonie. He carries on like his old self, still full of laughs and fun, and these men would kiss the ground he walks on. But he don't fool me. He's got a worm buried down there in his chest."

"Let it go, Hugh."

"You know his wife and both his children died of cholera?"

"Let's find that ammunition wagon and make sure everything's ready for tonight. They didn't have much power to spare, but they give us a lot of flints and a mess of nails."

"I told you I ain't done drinking yet."

"Listen, damn you, we're going to be moving at night, and for all we know there's Mexican skirmishers already out in them hills. How'd you like to run into one of their patrols while your brains was still boiled?"

"How much money you got?"

"About a dollar and a half and some scrip."

"Come on down to the river with me."

Son began to eat again without answering.

"When we get back to camp Burnett is going to have us digging shit holes till this war is over," Hugh said.

"I ain't going to no jenny-barn."

"You're still stuck on Sana, ain't you?"

"Maybe."

"You still figuring on going back there?"

"I ain't got no other place to go. You ain't, either."

"Listen, boy, it's no good to go back where you already been. It ain't the same. Other people own it, and it ain't yours no more."

"Come on," Son said.

"Where?"

"I'll ride down with you to that first cantina on the river and we'll have a drink. Then I'll buy you a meal and we'll find the ammunition wagon."

"I already know where it's at, and I'll put the cork in the jug when I feel like it. I done told you whiskey or wine don't bother me. If I can do a job sober, I can do it drunk, too."

"I understand that, Hugh, but how about taking your sleeve out of my plate?"

They went outside and rode through the cobbled streets toward a low adobe building on the river bank. Son looked across the river at the long gray walls of the Alamo Mission, the huge expanse of dirt plaza, the roofless crumbling church in the center, and wondered what it would be like to be trapped inside while thousands of Santa Anna's troops walked through their own cannon smoke, across their own dead, wave after wave, until they finally breached the wall and poured inside in a murderous mob. But this afternoon the sun was high above the hills in a blue sky, the mission was empty and quiet in the clear air, and the wind blew through the cattails on the river's edge and ruffled the green current and carried with it the laughter of girls in the cantina.

"Did you ask Bowie about Emile Landry?" Son said.

"What?"

"Get your mind off them tavern maids. What did Bowie say about Landry?"

"About two months ago he heered there was some slave hunters in town looking for two convicts. But he ain't seen no Frenchmen except the ones he brung over from Louisiana."

They left that night with the ammunition wagon for Gonzales. Going along the trace in the dark, Deaf said he had ridden fifteen miles into the hills south of town and had found a dead fire with a Mexican horseshoe in the ash.

CHAPTER
SIX

They were standing picket on the edge of the woods in the early dawn, and the fog hung in a solid white cloud on the meadow. They heard the rider before they saw him. Son and Hugh lifted their rifles to port arms, then the rider burst through the fog, his horse and clothes soaked with dew, his flop hat blowing behind his neck on a leather cord. Son heard a picket down the line cock his rifle.

"He's one of ours!" Son shouted.

The rider never slowed down. He bent low over the horse's neck and galloped through the trees, exploding ashes out of dead camp fires and clattering metal pots across the ground.

"Come back, you crazy sonofabitch," Son yelled after him.

"Let's get him before we have to explain how we let him through," Hugh said. They ran through the woods after the rider, and other men were crawling out of their tents and lean-tos.

"Shit, too late," Hugh said.

The rider had already stopped in front of Houston's tent, dropped the reins to the ground, and dismounted in one motion. Corporal Burnett was striding toward him angrily.

"General, I come from Bexar with a letter from Colonel Travis," the rider said outside the closed flap. He was breathless, and the backs of his legs were shaking from the long ride.

"General Houston ain't here," the corporal said. "What do you mean going through our camp like that?"

"Where's he at?"

"Washington-on-the-Brazos."

"Damn!" the rider said, then wiped the sweat off his forehead with the flat of his hand. There was almost pain in his eyes.

"You can talk with Captain Sherman. He's in the next tent."

"This letter goes to Houston."

"He's too far away for you."

"Colonel Travis said—"

"You done the best you could, soldier," the corporal said.

The captain untied his tent flap and held it partly open with his arm.

"Bring the letter in," he said.

The rider hesitated, then stooped under the canvas, and the captain tied the thong to the tent pole again.

"I got a notion Jim's luck has done run out," Hugh said.

"Look at that horse's sides. He must have roweled him all the way from Bexar," Son said.

The area around Captain Sherman's tent was now crowded with soldiers. Some of them were still pulling on their gum coats and tucking their pants inside their boots.

"What the hell you all think you're doing?" the corporal said. "The captain's talking, and he don't need nobody eavesdropping on him."

But no one moved.

"Go on, the lot of you," the corporal said.

"Are they caught over in Bexar?" one soldier said.

"How do I know?"

"You reckon we're marching?" another soldier said.

"I don't know nothing," the corporal said. "You all just get your ass back where you belong."

But they still didn't move. The sun began to burn through the fog, and a pale light filled the woods. Back in the trees the cooks were frying fatback on the Dutch oven.

The captain and the rider came out of the tent together.

"Corporal, get this man some breakfast and call muster in a half hour," the captain said, then went inside the tent again.

The soldiers followed Corporal Burnett and the rider in a large balloon to the cooking area. The rider sat on a log with a plate of fatback and cornbread in his hands and started to eat. They saw the exhaustion in his face and the way his thighs still quivered, and they waited for him to speak. But he simply continued to eat with his face turned into the plate.

"Don't bust your teeth on that cornbread. We use it for grapeshot sometimes," one soldier said in the silence.

"It's all right," the rider said. He wiped the grease off his mouth on his sleeve and started chewing on another piece of fatback. "Can one of you boys put my saddle on a fresh horse? I'm leaving out soon as I finished this."

"What's going on in Bexar?" Hugh said.

"We're surrounded. There must be thousands of them out there, and more is coming in every day. Santa Anna run a red flag up on a church, and his buglers is blowing the *Deguello*. They ain't giving no quarter."

"How'd you get out?" Son said.

"I was talking a little bit to Jesus, mister. I was almost through their line when I run right over about five of them sleeping on the ground. I could hear them balls popping around my ears."

"How'd you get surrounded?" another soldier said.

"Bowie probably didn't have no patrols out, that's how," the corporal said.

"It wouldn't make no difference. Bowie wouldn't run nohow," the rider said.

"Ain't you got no help from Fannin?"

"Far as I know he's still playing with himself down at Goliad. Davy Crockett come in, though, with twelve others from Tennessee. That sonofabitch don't know what scared is. He stands out there on the wall and pops Mexicans like turkeys and don't even duck down when he reloads."

"How many you lost?" Hugh said.

"Nobody. But them eighteen-pounders is knocking the hell out of the walls. That's the way the Mexicans fight. They get the edge on you and light a fire under your balls."

"I reckon we'll give them something else to think about when we come up their ass," another soldier said.

"I hope you do it soon. When they punch a couple of holes in our wall, they're going to come at us like flies swarming out of shit."

A young soldier led a fresh horse with the rider's saddle on it into the clearing. The rider set his plate on the edge of the Dutch oven and brushed his fingers on his coat.

"I'll see you boys later," he said. "You're right about the cornbread. You could knock a man unconscious with it."

"You going to find Houston?"

"One of you boys is going to do that. I'm headed back to the mission."

"You won't get through again," the corporal said.

"If I don't, them Mexicans is going to think they was attacked in the rear by the whole Texas army."

They watched him mount his horse, and each of them looked intently at his face.

"Hold on and I'll walk with you to the edge of the trees," Hugh said. "You can't never tell when you're going to step into a latrine around here."

He and Son walked along beside the rider to the edge of the field. The rider already had the reins wrapped around the back of his hand and was looking into the distance.

"How's Jim Bowie?" Hugh said.

"Real bad. He was setting a cannon up on the wall, the carriage toppled, and he took a hell of a fall. I think it busted his ribs. Right now they got him on a cot in the barracks. He can't hardly lift his head sometimes."

"Tell him you seen Hugh Allison."

"Sure."

"Here's a couple of twists of tobacco to chew on."

The rider put the tightly twisted leaves in his coat pocket.

"I'll see you all in Bexar," he said, and cut his Mexican spurs into the horse's ribs.

"What a time for Houston to be back on the Brazos," Son said.

"It don't make no difference."

"You reckon it's that bad?"

"We can't help them. They're on their own."

Ten minutes later they assembled for muster in the field, and the expectation was like electricity in each row of soldiers. They pulled on the cords of their powder horns and shifted their rifles from one hand to the other while the corporal called off the endless roll of names. The captain wore a blue high-collar uniform with brass buttons and braid on the shoulders, and his lean aristocratic features and educated Kentucky accent made Son vaguely distrustful of him.

"He don't look like he knows what he's going to say," he whispered.

"He's going to say what General Sam told him to say if this happened," Hugh said.

"That we're going to flesh out some Mexicans," a man behind them said.

"Shut up that talking in ranks," the corporal said.

The captain glanced briefly over the heads of the men, then began speaking as though he were choosing each word from a private box in his mind.

"Bexar is under siege. Santa Anna has moved anywhere from fifteen hundred to six thousand troops around the Alamo Mission. Some of them are *zapadores*, the best in the Mexican army, and their artillery is well placed beyond the range of our sharpshooters. However, Colonel Travis has written that he has been joined by Davy Crockett and his Tennessee volunteers."

"I can't hear him," the man behind Son said.

"Then be quiet," Son said.

"Many of you have been to Bexar and have seen the mission. It has thick walls on four sides, a deep well, and Colonel Travis has mounted cannon on top of the church. Also, he was able to put away a large store of food, powder, and shot before he was encircled. There is no better place that he could defend against such superior numbers.

"Many of us have lifelong friends within those walls. Everything in us urges us to go immediately to the aid of our countrymen. But not only is the fate of Bexar at stake now. The fate of Texas itself rests in our hands and what we do now. If we move on the Mexicans with our present force, we may bring relief temporarily to the Alamo, but we stand no chance of turning about the eventual outcome of the battle. By advancing from the Guadalupe we will open the entirety of south Texas to invasion, pillage, and defeat. There will be nothing to stop the barbarism of the Mexicans from here to the Sabine River.

"General Houston has been at the convention at Washington-on-the-Brazos. He is presently calling men to arms throughout the countryside. I expect him back in the next few days with a large and well-equipped force. By that time Colonel Fannin should be within striking distance of Bexar. In the meantime, we must all have faith in the stout hearts of our friends, who will hold the mission long beyond the limits of ordinary men. I know the pain that each of you feels at our situation, but we cannot allow a lack of forbearance to make worthless the courageous stand of those in the Alamo in our country's gravest hour. I ask each of you, separately, to stay here with me on the Guadalupe until General Houston's return."

After they were dismissed they continued to stand in the field, at first silent and numb, and then with a swelling anger that had no place to vent itself. Some of them looked meanly at the captain's back as he walked toward the trees, others stared toward the west as though they could catch sight of the cannon smoke drifting above the mission seventy miles away, and a few already had a bitter resolve in their faces that was impervious to an officer's rhetoric.

"It's our damn luck we got to stand picket again tonight," Hugh said.

"Let's see if we can go somewhere with Deaf and get out of it."

"He left last night for Victoria."

"Then let's make sure we're on the east side of the woods tonight."

"You know Burnett ain't going to let us off that easy."

That evening, while they ate their dinner by the fire, Son and Hugh saw several men go into their tents and lean-tos and begin rolling their blankets and few belongings inside their gum coats.

"Burnett stuck us on the west side of the woods tonight," Hugh said, loudly. "The wind off that river is colder than a well digger's ass."

"Turn in the other direction and you won't feel it," a voice inside a tent said.

There was a full moon that night, and the waving grass in the field was lighted with silver and the river was bright in the distance. Son and Hugh stood just inside the edge of the trees, with their rifles leaned against a pine trunk and their hands in their pockets. There were dark clouds in the west and a rain ring had formed around the moon.

"Who'd they put on the horses?" Son said.

"A couple of them fellows from Alabama. But I seen one of them roll his blankets after supper."

"Maybe they won't try it till tomorrow night."

"Shit, I hope so. Before this war's over I'm going to get even with Burnett for all the things he done to us."

"He's standing picket, too."

"Right. Down by the widest part of the river where nobody except a crazy man would try to cross."

"I can't hardly blame them fellows."

"Maybe I can't, either. But they're dead men when they leave here. And every man we lose is one less rifle when we get into it ourself."

"I heered the captain tell the lieutenant they was going to fire a cannon every morning in the mission to show they was still defending."

"That sounds like Travis. Jim wouldn't waste no powder setting off a gun that nobody except Mexicans will hear."

A long strip of black cloud slipped across the moon, and the field and the river were suddenly dark. Son and Hugh could hear their own breathing.

"Listen. There's somebody back there in the trees," Son said.

They stared through the black trunks of the pines, and the limbs overhead clicked against one another in the wind.

"I hope somebody ain't taking a piss back there, because I'd sure hate to shoot his pecker off," Hugh called out.

It was quiet a moment, then they heard movement in the trees again, this time going away from them.

"How are those dumb bastards going to get through the Mexican lines when they can't get past their own pickets?" Hugh said.

"I think they figured us for an easy mark. You know who's on picket up the line? That wild sonofabitch that shot a cow the other day."

"They figured wrong, then. I'll be damned if I'm going to get my ass turned on a spit. I already dug enough latrines for the whole country to shit in. And this deal could mean a court martial."

"You see him? Right the other side of that short pine."

In the dark they saw a man come out from the trees, holding his horse by the bridle and covering the nose with his other hand.

The man stood motionless in dark silhouette, then led his horse on into the field. A moment later fourteen other soldiers and horses followed him.

"Sonsofbitches," Hugh said. "I'd like to kill them. I should have beat the piss out of a couple of them earlier to get the message across."

"They're going to go right north of Burnett, and he's going to know where they come out."

"Look at them, strung out all the way across the field like a parade."

"What do you want to do?"

"Give them another minute. I reckon that ought to be enough even for these dumb assholes."

They waited silently while the column of men and horses went deeper into the field.

"All right," Hugh said. "Aim to the side. In case Burnett sees the flashes he can't tell us we shot high."

They let off their rifles, and the flames exploded out from the barrels into the darkness. A second later other pickets to the north and south of them fired their weapons, but the flashes were all at an upward angle. The column bolted for the river, each man bent low over his horse, his blanket roll bouncing behind the saddle.

"Good luck," Hugh said.

"I'll be damned. They went past Burnett and he didn't shoot."

"He's probably setting in his own shit. But then maybe he ain't all sonofabitch after all."

On the same day that Houston arrived back in camp, two Mexicans rode in and said that the mission had fallen. Before Houston could take the two men into his tent and question them, the news had already spread throughout the camp that there was now nothing to stop Santa Anna's advance across Texas. Houston placed the Mexicans under arrest and had his officers walk among the tents saying they were spies and their word was worthless, but that night twenty men who had families between Bexar and the Guadalupe swam their horses across the river.

It was barely first light when Deaf squatted before the lean-to and pulled on Son's boot.

"Get in the saddle," he said. "You ain't got time to eat. Just put some biscuits in your poke."

"What's going on?" Hugh said.

"We're riding as close to Bexar as we can."

"Now, wait a minute, Deaf," Hugh said.

"I ain't got time to talk with you. Just get it moving."

"There might be a few thousand Mexicans down that road."

"That's right, and we ain't going to get caught with our britches hanging in a tree."

"I thought them Mexicans was supposed to be spies," Son said.

"Spies, my ass. They're a couple of farmers," Deaf said.

They forded the river on a submerged pebble-covered sandbar and rode up through the willows on the other side. It had rained during the night, but now the sky was a clear blue with pink clouds on the horizon and they could feel the early sun on their backs. The live oaks and the blackjack and the grass in the fields were shining with dew, and the rolling countryside ahead looked so beautiful to Son that it seemed impossible to believe that down the trace the mission could be a fire-blackened ruin and all the soldiers he had met in Bexar were dead.

"Deaf, what do you reckon Houston's going to do if them two Mexicans was right?" he said.

"He already told me. Put a rear guard on Gonzales to get the civilians out and run."

"When the hell do we stop?"

"When we ain't got to fight them like they want us to. That's what Fannin can't understand. Sam's ordered him to haul his ass to Victoria before he gets cut up, too. But if I know Fannin he'll still be thinking about taking Matamoros when the grape starts singing around his ears."

"You still ain't answered me."

"No, and I ain't got to. Maybe the whole army will get chewed up in pieces before we can turn and make them hurt. But if they can be whupped with what we got, Sam will find the way to do it."

"We ain't arguing with you, Deaf," Hugh said. "It just don't feel too good to run."

"He knows that. It don't feel good to him, either. Some of them sonsofbitches back at Washington-on-the-Brazos is calling him a drunkard and a coward."

"That ain't all he's going to get called when them back at camp hear we're running," Son said.

"Them kind ain't worth a shit nohow, and I just as lief be shut of them," Deaf said.

That afternoon, as they came out of an oak grove, they saw a white woman and a black man coming toward them on horseback. A second black man walked beside them, and the woman held a little girl in her arms. Her dress was gathered up to her thighs so she could ride like a man, and there was a soiled bandage on her leg. Her clothes were spotted with dried mud, her face windburned, and there was an electric quality in her face that a person with a high fever would have.

"Do you come from Bexar, ma'am?" Deaf said.

She continued to stare at him strangely.

"She don't understand Deaf's voice," Son said.

"You're coming from Bexar, ain't you, ma'am?" Hugh said.

"Yes. They are all killed there."

"Well, you let me hold that little girl a piece. I bet your arms is plumb wore out," Hugh said.

He dismounted and started to take the child from her, but her arms were rigid.

"It's all right. We're with Sam Houston's army at Gonzales," he said. "We're going to rest a bit and then take you there."

"Why didn't you come? They waited on the walls for you each morning."

"Let's go back to the trees where you can rest," Hugh said, with the child on his shoulder. "I got some biscuits in my poke, and I'm going to warm them up for this little one."

"Where's Santa Anna at?" Deaf said to the black man on horseback.

"They coming on the trace. We seen their fires way off one night."

"How many fires?"

The man shook his head.

"Was there a lot or just a few?"

The man was afraid to answer. Instead, he reached inside his shirt and handed Deaf a waxen brown envelope sealed with a melted candle. As they rode back toward the oak trees Deaf opened the letter in his fingers.

"It's in Spanish," Son said.

"That's because it's from Santa Anna himself. Wait till Sam sees this."

"What's it say?"

"He'll pardon any Texian that lays down his arms. Otherwise, we all get the same they got at the Alamo."

"I reckon the general will find a use for that paper," Hugh said.

Hugh built a fire of twigs in the trees and browned his biscuits on a sharpened stick for the woman and the little girl. The woman said her name was Susannah Dickerson, the wife of Lieutenant Almeron Dickerson, one of the last to die in the mission. Then she told the story of the eleven-day siege and the final attack at dawn on March 6 that left all one hundred and eighty-eight Texians dead and fifteen hundred Mexican casualties.

The Mexican artillery pounded the walls for days, and each time a breach was made and the Texians had to repair it the Mexicans loaded with grape and moved their cannon closer until they were less than three hundred yard from the plaza. The sharpshooters on the wall devastated the Mexican infantry whenever they tried to move their line forward, but the barrage continued without respite through the day, and each night there were more and more campfires surrounding the mission as Santa Anna received re-enforcements. The plaza was filled with craters and strewn with exploded rubble, and by the afternoon of March 5 the smoke was so thick from the Mexican cannons that the Texians could barely see the thousands of troops waiting on four sides of them.

Travis assembled the men and told them that no help was coming, their hours were probably short, and that any man who wished could surrender and ask for quarter or try to get through the Mexican lines. That night a man named Louis Rose dropped over the north wall.

As the first light touched the hills the next morning they heard the *Deguello* blow, then the Mexicans attacked in waves as far as the eye could see. The Texians loaded their cannons with chopped horseshoes, nails, and trace chains, and cut huge holes in the Mexican advance. But their ranks closed again, and they kept coming through the smoke with their bayonets fixed while the gunners on top of the church worked furiously to depress their cannon and reload.

The sharpshooters on the wall fired pointblank into the Mexicans'

faces and clubbed and stabbed at their heads and threw back their
ladders. Then the earthen works by the church were blown apart
and they poured into the plaza, screaming with the adrenaline of
having lived through the initial attack. Travis was dead with a ball
through the brain, and Crockett and the other survivors from the
walls were running for the barracks by the church. The gunners
on top of the church turned their cannon around and fired into
the breached earthen works. The Mexicans caught there were
shredded with hundreds of nails. Then the breach was filled with
screaming men again, and the gunners were cut down with a
fusillade of rifle balls as they tried to swab out their cannon with
buckets of water.

Crockett and three others were hacked to pieces against the
barracks wall. The Mexicans burst through the barracks door and
found Jim Bowie on his cot. He fired a derringer into the face
of a sergeant, then a dozen bayonets entered his body almost
simultaneously.

When the shooting had stopped the Mexicans found five Texians
who had tried to hide. They were taken before Santa Anna and
then executed. The bodies of the Texians were stacked in the
plaza, with mesquite brush under each layer of dead, and burned.
The fire lasted until morning, and a sweet-sickening smell hung
over Bexar for two days.

That night they broke camp on the Guadalupe and began to
retreat eastward. They spiked two brass cannons and sank them
in the river, loaded their wagons until the wheel rims sank to the
spokes in the sand, and put a rear guard on Gonzales to protect
the civilian evacuation. The rear guard was told to burn any supplies
that could be used by the Mexicans, but instead they burned the
whole town. The long column of horses, wagons, soldiers on foot,
and escaping families wound through the dark woods, creek beds,
and flooded bottoms, and Houston rode up and down the line,
talking quietly to frightened children, calling men who had enlisted
only a few days earlier by name, and dismounting to push on a
wagon when it became mired in a slough. Throughout the night
they could still see the glow of the fires in Gonzales. Toward dawn
Houston noticed that the last supply wagon in the column had
fallen far back in the rear and that the riders around it were swaying
in the saddle.

"Allison and Holland, come with me," he said.

They galloped along the column to the wagon. The two team-sters in the wagon-box had been members of the rear guard, and their eyelids were half-shut and their faces white. The riders were in equally bad condition, grinning and nodding stupidly at Houston.

"I see you gentlemen managed to save the whiskey before you burned the town," he said.

"We figured they'd be sick people that could use it, General," one rider said.

"I'm glad you men had the welfare of others in mind. Now chop up all those barrels."

"Some of it's Spanish rum, General."

"That's good. Only the best should go into the soil of the republic."

Hugh dismounted, picked up a barrel over his head, and smased the staves apart against a rock.

"My heart's leaking, too, boys," he said. "That smell sure does bring back a lot of wonderful nights, don't it?"

They burst barrels all over the ground and trees until their moccasins and boots were soaking in liquor. Houston watched from his horse with a handkerchief contianing hartshorn held to his nose. Hugh was laughing, his face and hair beaded with drops of whiskey.

"Is it that bad, General?" he said.

"I'm afraid that it is, Hugh."

For two weeks the retreat continued, through Burnham's Cross-ing, Beason's Ferry, San Felipe, and finally to Groce's Landing on the Brazos River. Houston refused to tell his men or even his junior officers when he planned to turn and fight, and at night the anger and the doubt toward him grew around the camp fires.

Then two riders came into camp and told what happened to James Fannin and his men at Goliad.

They had been caught in the open six miles out of town by one thousand of General Urrea's troops. They overturned their wagons, shot their horses for cover, threw up earthen works, and fought for two days without water until they were pulling nails from their wagon boards to fire in their muskets. Fannin surrendered, and was told that his men would be paroled, marched to the coast, and placed on a ship for New Orleans.

"It was early Palm Sunday morning when they come in the presidio and started picking up our blankets," one of the riders said. He was a tall mountain man dressed in buckskin, with an old scar across his nose and two fingers missing from his right hand. "We should have figured then what they was up to. I asked this one Mexican to let me keep my blanket, and he said you won't need it no more. They marched three hundred and fifty of us out on the road, and left Colonel Fannin and about seventy other wounded in the presidio. Just before I went out the gate I seen the colonel setting by a fire with a stick twisted through the bandage on his leg. He said, 'Don't you worry none, Will. We'll be having a drink together in New Orleans next week.'

"All along the road there was Mexican women saying, 'Pobrecitos. Pobrecitos.' Then them sonsofbitches told us to kneel down. The fellow next to me says, 'I'll be damned if I'll kneel before a greaser,' and then somebody hollers, 'Run for it, boys. They're going to shoot us.' Their guns was going off all around us. They was firing so close to us I could feel the powder stinging my skin. People was crying out to Jesus and hunched up on the ground with their arms over their heads. The face of that boy next to me just exploded all over my chest. I don't know how I done it, but I run right over a Mexican and kept on a-going till I hit the woods. Behind me they was gigging the wounded with their pig stickers. I could hear them screaming a half mile into the trees.

"About an hour later I heered shooting start again back at the presidio. It didn't last long this time, though. Most of them poor boys was already hurt so bad they couldn't do nothing but lie there."

Houston heard that Santa Anna was preparing to cross the Brazos south of him, and he sent Deaf, Son, and Hugh down the river toward Fort Bend. Spring was taking hold of the land; the new grass was green in the fields, and the first wild flowers grew along the creek banks. The mornings were still cool, but by noon the sun was warm, and there was a smell in the air of pine rosin and plowed acreage.

At San Felipe they picked up the rutted wagon and hoof tracks of the Mexican advance, but because the Mexicans marched in a long double file and had been driving cattle with them, it was impossible to estimate the size of their force. North of Fort Bend, they entered a pine woods on a low crest above the river, and Deaf swung down from his horse and felt the ashes in a dead camp fire.

"They ain't far," he said. "Let's walk them. Don't shoot at nothing, even if you step on one's face."

"I don't know about that, Deaf," Son said.

"You drop a hammer in here and you won't live fifteen minutes. You ever kill a man with a knife?"

"I have," Hugh said. "There ain't nothing to it. You just give it to them in the rib cage, twist once, and you're out."

"Good," Deaf said.

They walked on through the woods, leading their horses, and down the slope they could see the Brazos floating high over its banks into the willow trees. Deaf stopped raised his hand, and remained motionless. Then he turned, held up two fingers, and tethered his horse to a pine trunk. Neither Son nor Hugh could see anything through the trees. They stooped low and crept forward over the pine needles, with Deaf in the lead. Son smelled tobacco smoke.

In a short clearing they saw two Mexican privates with their backs turned to them. They had leaned their muskets against a tree, and one of them was smoking a pipe. They were watching a flatboat on the river that was out of control in the current. Deaf pulled his bowie knife out of the deerskin scabbard on his leg and pointed at the Mexican on the right for Hugh and Son. Then they crashed out of the brush together into the clearing.

Deaf drove his knife all the way to the hilt into the back of the picket's neck so that the point came out the throat. A bloody clot exploded from the picket's mouth, his body shook in a convulsion, and he slipped forward off the knife as though he had been disemboweled. The second man had been quicker when he heard the brush rattle, and had run for his musket. Hugh swung his knife at him, but the man arched his back away from the blade and the point caught only the cloth of his jacket. But Son ran toward him at the same time with his rifle butt held up like a pike and drove it into the man's ear. The man spun around in a pirouette, off balance, and Son hit him twice more as though he were hammering a nail into wood.

"Go down, you sonofabitch," he said.

Deaf stabbed his knife into the picket's back and lifted on the handle at the same time.

"Take their guns. They can use them back at camp," he said.

"Them Mexicans sure got hard heads, ain't they?" Hugh said.

Son was still breathing hard.

"I wonder why he didn't holler out," he said.

"He was too scared," Hugh said.

"These is probably their furtherest pickets," Deaf said. "That means their camp is about four or five hundred yards away. If we run across any more pickets, we ain't going to jump them. We'll go around from the other side."

They worked their way on through the woods, staying close to the pine trunks, their heads bent low, and stopping like pieces of stone whenever they heard a pine cone topple through the branches overhead to the ground. They saw the trees begin to thin ahead, and they circled away from the river until they reached an eroded gulley, with heavy timber on each side, that led back toward the river bank.

They walked along the edge of the gulley through the wild fern and deep shadows, and they could smell the dank, cool odor of the water coursing over the rocks below; then they saw the sunlight at the end of the trees where the stream bed sloped down to the Brazos. They crawled on their stomachs until they could look out over the wide stretch of sandy bank.

"Look at all them bastards," Hugh said.

The bank was covered with Mexican troops, tents, horses, mules, oxen, and ammunition and supply wagons. A ferry boat loaded with infantry was crossing the river. In the center of the camp was a command tent with the Mexican tricolor flag flying over it.

Deaf took a spy glass from inside his shirt and moved it slowly back and forth over the beach as though he were dividing it into segments that he could reduce to numerical equations in his mind. Then he handed Son the glass, took a piece of slate from his shirt pocket, and began making columns of tally marks.

"You check me," he said. "I count fifteen wagons. Most of them look like ammunition. Which means they're living off the land. Which means they're stealing and burning everything as they go. I don't see but one field piece down there, and it looks like a twelve-pounder. Some of that infantry is *zapadores*, and that means this is probably the same bunch that killed everybody in the Alamo. I think Sam will be glad to hear that little piece of news. Now, I just need to find out if that little fart Santa Anna is in that tent yonder.

But as Son looked through the glass, he wasn't thinking of the number of troops, cannon, or ammunition wagons in the camp. He had focused the lens on five men who were drinking from cups at a table under a canvas awning.

"Take a look, Hugh. Just to the right of the command tent."

Hugh put his good eye to the glass.

"Sonofabitch. He's still with it," he said.

"I thought he'd throw it in by this time."

"We should have doubled back on them bastards and cut their throats months ago."

"What's wrong with you two?" Deaf said.

"There's a fellow down there named Emile Landry and four others that's got a special interest in us," Hugh said.

"You mean them Louisiana prison guards?"

"How'd you know?" Son said.

"Sam told me. I don't take nobody out on scout with me unless I know what time of day he drops his britches."

"At least we can kill the sonofabitch now and not get hung for murder," Hugh said.

"You ain't going to do it today. And before you go thinking them men down yonder don't have nothing to do but chase you across Texas, remember you ain't the only ones in this army that got warrants on them from Louisiana. I think half of them Frenchies Bowie brung with him to Bexar had manacle scars on their ankles."

"That might be true, but that man's got something extra in mind for us," Son said.

"Then he done joined up with the wrong bunch, because Sam was mad as hell when he heered about what happened at Goliad, and when the time comes these Mexicans ain't going to get no more mercy than they give Jim Fannin."

When they got back to camp and reported to Houston's tent, they disovered that Santa Anna had sent a black man to the general with a message that he was going to burn the temporary capital at Harrisburg, execute anyone there bearing arms, then march on Houston's army and destroy it.

"I don't know whether to believe it or not. What do you think, Mr. E.?" Houston said to Deaf. He was pushed back in his chair with his boot on the table. Son and Hugh stood with their arms folded over their rifle barrels.

"He's an arrogant enough sonofabitch to do it," Deaf said.

"But you saw only one twelve-pounder. Would he attack with no more artillery than that to support him?"

"I ain't one to say, but I think they're getting careless, General," Hugh said. "If we'd had a field piece, we could have blowed grape all over their camp."

"Yes. Yes. But was that Santa Anna you saw on the river? We won't bring peace to Texas until we put our hand on his throat."

"I'da stayed there all day to find out, Sam, but we killed them two pickets and their relief was coming sometime."

"I know, Mr. E. I never had a better scout. You two fellows have done well by me, too," Houston said. He took a piece of shaved pine wood and a pocket knife from his coat and began to notch it between his thumb and the blade. "I'm just going to have to think on this one a bit."

That night they began the march to Harrisburg. More volunteers from east Texas had joined Houston's army, but many of the men had come down with measles and the worst thunderstorm of the spring drenched the prairie. The oxen and two six-pounder cannon, which Houston had named "the twin sisters of Texas," mired in the mud, the horses reared in the flashes of lightning across the sky, and the rain drove so hard in the men's eyes that they couldn't see a line of trees fifty yards before them. They marched for two and one-half days, sleeping in wet blankets and eating their food cold, to arrive at Buffalo Bayou and find Harrisburg burned and the government fled.

"Damn, the Mexicans don't leave much behind when they go through a place," Hugh said.

The stores, saloons, and shotgun houses along the dirt streets were still smoking in the light rain, and the people who had been driven out of town when the Mexicans set it afire had now returned and were pulling blackened boards loose from the piles of debris that had been their homes and businesses. An odor of burned hair and horseflesh still came from the livery stable, and the cattle in the lot behind the stock barn had all been shot.

"What they got against these people?" Son said.

"Nothing."

"Look at that old woman rooting in them busted preserve jars."

"That's the worst thing about a war. The civilians ain't got no stake in it, and they always get it first."

"Santa Anna better pray he ain't ever captured. I was listening last night to some boys that was at Goliad. They got some real mean things in their mind."

"Like Deaf says, he's such an arrogant sonofabitch he thinks he can torch the whole country and then cut us up for breakfast. We're going to find out pretty soon, though."

"How you know? Houston don't say shit half the time about what we're doing."

"The San Jacinto River is just east of us. I don't think him or Santa Anna either one wants to cross it this time of year. Besides, there's all kind of swamps on each side of it."

The army marched eastward, and the next day Son, Hugh, and Deaf rode ten miles ahead of the advance and encountered a Mexican patrol of fifteen mounted soldiers that had just emerged from a woods into a long open field. The Mexicans were stopped about two hundred yards away, staring at the three of them. Son pulled back the hammer of his rifle to half-cock.

"Don't shoot," Deaf said. "Wait till we see what they're going to do. They ain't sure what we got behind us."

An officer in the lead put a spy glass to his eye, then kicked his spurs into his horse's sides.

"He wants prisoners. Give it to them and shoot low," Deaf said.

They fired their rifles almost simultaneously, and clouds of black smoke exploded from their barrels. Two of the Mexican horses went down, but the other riders kept coming.

"Hit it for the trees!" Deaf said.

They jerked the reins around and poured it on their horses. Son was leaned forward in the saddle, the reins in his teeth, his legs clenched tightly on the horse's heaving sides, while he tried to pull the ramrod from his rifle. He heard three or four rifles go off behind him and then the popping sound of a ball cutting through the air by his ear. They thundered into the pine trees, swung down from their saddles, and crouched behind the trunks.

"Get that Colt working!" Deaf yelled. He and Son were pouring powder and ramming balls and greased patches down their rifle barrels.

Hugh knelt to the side of a pine tree and began firing and cocking the heavy Colt's revolver with both hands. Each time the hammer came down the gun roared upward over his head. The explosions were deafening. A red hole the size of a dollar burst open in a Mexican horse's forequarters, and the rider went down with him in a tangle of hooves and reins and stirrups.

"Ole spy glass there is going to think we got a regiment in here," Hugh said.

By the time his hammer clicked on an empty chamber, Son and Deaf were reloaded and aiming their Kentucky rifles at the crossed bandoliers on the officer's chest. Deaf fired first, and the ball caught the officer in the stomach and blew blood out his back on the horse's rump. The reins collapsed, the horse slowed to a walk, and the officer sat still in the saddle with his hands pressed to the wound as though he could hold his life inside him. The other Mexicans turned and raced back toward the opposite woods. The man who had lost his horse was running among them.

"Let's see what we got out here," Deaf said.

They walked into the field, where the officer still sat in the saddle. His eyes were caught between fear of them and his death.

"Donde está Santa Anna?" Deaf said.

The Mexican's head nodded forward, and the movement caused his horse to walk a few paces until Son took the reins.

"This fellow ain't no good to us. Go through his saddle bags," Hugh said.

Deaf untied his saddle bags and emptied them on the ground. They held a pair of socks and underwear, a shirt, a bar of soap and a razor, some women's hose, and a heavy gold watch.

Deaf unsnapped the gold case on the watch and read the inscription inside: "To Our Beloved Son, David Cummings."

"What's the matter?" Hugh said.

"I knowed this man in Bexar."

Hugh and Son were silent a moment.

"What d' you want to do with spy glass here? He's fading pretty fast," Hugh said.

"Pull his wood tag and leave him. We need to find out what's on the other side of that woods. A patrol this big means they ain't far from home."

Through the humid afternoon and evening they continued to scout the perimeter of Santa Anna's army. Late that night when they reported back to Houston, Deaf said he was convinced that Santa Anna was turning his troops north at San Jacinto Bay, which would put him in a box with the water at his back.

Santa Anna camped on a stretch of dry elevated ground on the southeast side of the river, with a large marsh area on his right flank. His engineers built breastworks of logs and earth on his front and left flank, and the twelve-pounder cannon was placed in the center of the line so that it could command the open field.

Less than a mile to the north Houston had moved his troops into a thick woods and had placed his six-pounder cannon on the edge of the trees. On the afternoon of April 21 Houston assembled the soldiers and addressed them from horseback. The men were crowded together in the trees, their long rifles butt-down on the ground, pistols and knives stuck in their belts, flags furled on their staffs.

Son looked around him.

"Where's Deaf at?" he said, because Deaf was never far from Houston unless he was scouting, and there was no need for a scout now.

"I seen him and Burnett ride out with a pair of axes this morning," Hugh said.

"Up that rise waits the usurper and fifteen hundred of his troops," Houston said. "They outnumber us two to one, but they have never been attacked before and they do not expect us to do it now. It is three-fifteen, they are in their siesta, and our attack will catch them in disarray. Each of us knows what will happen if we are not victorious today. The Mexicans will sweep through east Texas and devastate the colonies with torch and sword. They must not leave the field. Remember the Alamo, remember Goliad, and think of the fate of our loved ones if the usurper is not destroyed this afternoon. As civilized men we have followed the ways of mercy,

even in war, but they must not be allowed to spend one more day
at their evil design on our soil. If your heart is faint at what we
must do, remember the Alamo. Let that be your cry when you meet
those who ask for what they never gave themselves. Remember the
Alamo. Remember the Alamo. Remember the Alamo."

The lines of infantry formed on the edge of the woods, and the
cavalry under Colonel Sherman and Mirabeau Buonaparte Lamar
moved out on the flanks. The sunlight was dazzling on the field,
and a warm breeze was blowing off the river. Houston gave orders
that no one was to fire until told to do so, and no one was to
shout out until the enemy was actually engaged. The flags were
unfurled, the rifles pulled back to half-cock, and a fifer and drummer
stood immobile behind the switching tail of Houston's horse. Then
Houston waved his hat forward, and the line advanced while the
drummer and fifer played "Will You Come to the Bower I Have
Shaded for You?"

Son's mouth was dry and his hands made wet stains on his rifle
stock. He didn't know if what he felt inside him was fear or
expectation, but when he tried to focus his eyes through the haze
on the Mexican camp and the field piece he knew was on the top
of the rise, beads of sweat distorted his vision and made the whole
field shimmer with refracted light. He ran his thumb over the flint
screwed in his hammer and wondered if the edge was too thin and
would break when it struck the steel by the flashpan. He had
prayed seldom since he went to prison, but now the words to the
"Our Father" came disjointedly to his mind. There was not a sound
from the field except the song of the fifer and drummer. He looked
at Hugh's face, and it was gray and as tight as a drumhead.

"Why ain't they shot yet?" he said. His words were full of phlegm.

"Don't worry. It's going to come at us like somebody opened
the door to hell," the rider next to him said.

Then the Mexican twelve-pounder roared on top of the rise,
lurching upward on its carriage in a cloud of dust, and a cannon
ball arched *whooshing* out of its trajectory overhead and crashed
into the woods behind them. A gunner poured water from a wooden
bucket down the barrel, and another man rammed the swabbing
rod inside. Puffs of musket smoke exploded from the breastworks
and drifted out into the field, and beyond Son's line of vision he
could hear the Mexicans yelling in camp. The gunners loaded

another twelve-pound ball with a powder sack attached to it and were screwing down the elevation on the cannon.

Oh God, we're going into it point-blank, Son thought.

Out of the corner of his eye he saw Deaf galloping across the field with an axe held above his head.

"Vince's Bridge is down. Vince's Bridge is down," he shouted.

"There ain't no way out of here now," Hugh said.

The cannon roared again, and this time Son could see the wave of heat flatten the grass in front of the barrel's mouth. Behind him a geyser of dirt exploded into the air, and a rider and his horse were left twisted and quivering on the edge of the crater. The breastworks were no more than sixty yards away now, and the Mexicans were firing and reloading furiously in relays. Musket balls popped and crisscrossed through the air, and the gunners were ramming grape down the cannon barrel.

The man next to Son had his reins clipped in half by a ball. He stared at the slack leather in his hand, then as he looked quizzically at the breastworks a rose petal burst between his eyes, his jaw fell open, and he toppled sideways from the saddle onto Son's horse.

"All right, give it to them," Houston yelled. "Infantry kneel and fire. Kneel and fire. Remember the Alamo! Remember Goliad!"

The first line of infantry knelt and fired a ragged volley into the breastworks, and a second line rushed into place beside them, knelt in the grass and fired, while the first reloaded. Then they rushed screaming up the slope into the Mexican guns.

Son and Hugh were with Lamar's cavalry, and they charged the Mexican flank by the marsh. As Son's horse labored up the incline, he could see the faces of the Mexicans in the smoke behind the breastworks. They were terrified. They were firing too fast and shooting high, and some of them had already started running for the rear. He threw his rifle to his shoulder, aimed at a soldier who was rising from his knees, and pulled the trigger. The ball tore through the soldier's chest, then Son felt his horse's hooves clatter over the logs and piled dirt at the top of the embankment.

"Holland's inside! Damn it, get over the top with him! Ride right over them!" he heard Lamar shout behind him.

The Mexican camp was chaos. Many of the Mexicans had been asleep when the first shots were fired, the cavalry had been watering their horses down by the river, and the ammunition wagons were

far back from the breastworks with no oxen yoked to them so that
a soldier had to run to the rear when he was out of ammunition.
Loose horses and mules galloped in panic through the camp, knocking down tents and stacked rifles and colliding into groups of
running men. The Texians poured over the breastworks, swinging
their rifles like axes and slashing at heads with swords and bowie
knives.

Son felt his horse go out from under him, and he fell headlong
on the body of a Mexican soldier. He knelt in the smoke, the
ramrod in his teeth, his hands shaking, and tried to pour powder
from his horn down the barrel. Thirty yards away he could see
two Mexicans aiming at him through the smoke. Then he heard
Hugh's Colt fire three times above him.

"You'll get killed trying to reload. Get your ass up here," Hugh
said.

Son put his foot in the loose stirrup and swung up on the horse's
rump. To their left they saw a Texian stand back from the Mexican
twelve-pounder and throw a burning piece of firewood behind it.
"That stupid sonofabitch is blowing the magazine," Hugh said.

The explosion blew a fountain of dirt, splintered logs, and parts
of the dead gunners fifty feet in the air. The cannon lurched forward
on its carriage and toppled down the slope.

"Start busting skulls. We're going right into them," Hugh said.

Hugh charged his horse into a group of fleeing Mexicans and
shot one man through the neck. Son swung his rifle by the barrel
with one hand, holding onto Hugh's waist with the other, and
caught a Mexican across the back of the head with the stock. The
man fell on his hands and knees, and Hugh jerked the reins around
and rode his horse over him.

The Mexicans who had fallen back from the breastworks were
now surrounded on all sides with the marsh at their backs. Others,
some barefoot, were running across the plain toward Vince's Bridge.
In the clouds of smoke and dust Son saw a man in pantaloons with
a head like a cannonball trying to catch up a horse that had a
slipped saddle on it.

"It's him," he said.

"Damn if it ain't!" Hugh sawed back the reins, cocked, aimed
the Colt with both hands, and yelled out at the same time: "Landry!
It's Hugh Allison!" Then he fired.

"You missed. Shoot again."

"I'm empty."

Hugh threw his leg over the horse's head and dropped to the ground. He tore a rifle out of the hands of a soldier who had just reloaded.

"What the hell are you doing?" the soldier said.

Hugh knelt on one knee and squeezed off the trigger into the drifting smoke. The recoil almost knocked him down. The shot was high, and Emile Landry swung onto the horse and raced down the far slope with the slipped saddle flopping under the horse's belly. Hugh threw the rifle against the soldier's chest.

"You dumb bastard. You must have put a half-horn in there," he said.

Mexicans were stumbling into the marsh, struggling against the sand and soft mud that sank them up to their knees. Many of them couldn't swim, and as they went deeper into the water toward the river they put their hands high in the air and begged for quarter. But the Texians waded after them, firing point-blank into their faces or bayoneting them as they tried to push away the Texian muskets with their hands. The screams from the marsh were terrible, and the water along the sandy bay was diffused with pink.

The command tent in the center of the camp was still standing. A soldier ripped down the Mexican tricolor flag from the staff and started to tear it under his foot.

"Don't do that," Lamar, the cavalry officer, said. "We'll save it for those who thought we were more jackrabbit than soldier."

He threw back the flap on the tent. The bedclothes were pulled halfway off the cot, and a small folding night table which had held a water pitcher, a bowl of fruit, and a diary had been knocked into the corner.

"It looks like Santa Anna had him a right expensive siesta," Hugh said.

"Well, he won't be hard to find. Just look for the fellow that forgot to put his britches on," Son said.

They walked back out the tent, and Lamar flung the flap to in disgust.

"Don't laugh, gentlemen," he said. "Everything we've done here means nothing if Santa Anna escapes from us now."

The shooting had almost stopped in the marsh, and bodies

whose uniforms were puffed with air floated in the dead current and hung in grotesque positions among the tree trunks. But the firing was still heavy on the plain where the Texians were chasing the Mexicans toward Vince's Bridge. Son and Hugh reloaded their weapons; Son caught up a saddled horse, and they rode down off the slope onto the plain with other cavalry toward Buffalo Bayou.

Green horseflies had already started to hum over the Mexican dead who were scattered over the ground for two miles. Son saw the barefoot body of a man in gray pantaloons and filthy white shirt lying face down in the grass. There was a deep saber slash through his back that exposed his ribs. Son dismounted and turned him over with his foot.

"You know him?" he said.

"I seen him once. He brought some boys into camp in the jail wagon."

"You two better stop thinking about looting and start popping some caps," a soldier next to them said. "Houston and Deaf are pushing a whole bunch of them back in the trees by the bayou."

A Mexican officer had gotten some control over his men and had formed them into a firing line on the edge of the woods. Son and Hugh galloped their horses into Houston's advancing line, and they could see dozens of Mexicans crouched behind the tree trunks and the dirty puffs of smoke that exploded into the sunlight and flattened in the breeze.

"Where the hell you been?" Deaf said.

"Trying to slip a pig-string on Santa Anna."

Houston's horse had five rifle holes in it, and there was a tear in his trousers and a long area of scarlet that ran down his leg.

"General, you're bleeding like a stuck hog," Hugh said.

"Move on the trees, boys. They're almost finished."

Then his horse collapsed under him. Deaf and Son were immediately on each side of him with their hands under his arms. They pulled him to his feet, and he held his leg stiffly off the ground as though it were set with a splint.

"Get me another horse and attack. Don't waver now. The field is ours."

Corporal Burnett, whose face was burned and puckered from a powder flash, brought up another horse, and they helped Houston into the stirrup.

"Set this one out, Sam. We'll push them into the water in fifteen minutes," Deaf said.

"Form to me! Form to me!" Houston shouted, waving his hat at the mounted men and infantry on each side of him. "Run them to the bayou, boys. They're too frightened to shoot straight now."

Then he whipped his hat on the horse's rump, and the line charged forward toward the trees. Son felt his shirt jump, and he looked down and saw a hole where a ball had passed through the cloth just above his old wound. Deaf was waving a Mexican broadsword over his head as though he were generating enough energy in his arm to fell a tree with a single stroke. Hugh was already firing his Colt, the explosions and splintered lead from the chambers singeing the hair on his horse's head. Just as they crashed through the underbrush on the edge of the trees, the Mexicans who still had loaded guns fired their last volley and ran for the bayou. A Mexican corporal was stumbling backward from Son, stabbing frantically at the horse with his bayonet. Son stood in the stirrups and fired downward, and the ball splintered the man's rifle stock apart in his hands and left him open-mouthed and atrophied with fear until Son's horse knocked him reeling into a tree.

The Mexicans who were not bayoneted or clubbed to the ground in the woods ran down the muddy bank of the bayou, splashed through the shallows, then fell suddenly into deep water where they thrashed their arms wildly against the pull of their bandoliers and tight jackets. Then the Texians emerged from the tree and took aim.

"Give quarter!" Houston shouted. "They're quit."

The soldiers lowered their rifles and looked back at him.

"Some of them out there is *zapadores*, General. They was at Bexar," one man said.

"They're now our prisoners," Houston said. "Deaf, ride to Vince's Bridge and give my order."

"They're going to be hard to stop, Sam."

"The order is to give quarter to all who lay down their arms."

"Tell them they better stop wasting shot on these assholes and catch that sonofabitch Santa Anna," Hugh said.

The Mexicans in the bayou were told in Spanish to wade ashore. Their eyes were wide with fright, and some of the Texians repeat-

edly cocked the hammers of their rifles. Deaf rode off toward the
firing that still came from Vince's Bridge. The Texians picked up
the Mexican weapons that were scattered through the woods and
marched their prisoners into the field. Son and Hugh were in the
rear, and a soldier in deerskin clothes with a Mexican sword in his
belt walked beside them. He was looking ahead at Houston and
chewing on a small twig in his mouth.

"I wonder if I ought to tell the general about it," he said.

"About what?" Son said.

"I killed a fellow back there that don't seem to belong here."

"Get that stick out of your mouth and make sense," Hugh said.

"He wasn't no soldier. Maybe he was a spy. I didn't have time
to pull out his pockets. A Mexican come out from behind a tree
and liked to took my head off with a rock."

"Show him to us," Son said.

"We're going to get separated from the others. This woods is
still full of half-crazy Mexicans."

"You can ride up with me. Where's he at?" Son said.

The soldier led them back through the trees to the bayou. They
saw the pantalooned legs of a man sticking out from behind a
willow tree toward the water's edge. The man was seated upright
against the trunk, his round head cleaved nearly in two. One palm
was turned upward on his thigh like a gargoyle's claw, and his
index finger was pointed outward in the same direction as his
empty eyes. A cap and ball pistol lay by his foot.

As Son looked at the destroyed face, he also saw the face of
the brother strangling above the chain that twisted into his throat.

"I run up on him out of the brush, and when I seen he wasn't
no soldier I was going to tell him to lay down on his stomach. But
he come up with a pistol, and I slit his skull. You reckon I ought
to tell Deaf or the general?"

"He don't mean nothing to nobody now. We done whupped
them," Hugh said.

"What'd you want to see him for, then?"

"You might have had Santa Anna there, boy," Hugh said. "But
this ain't him. I seen Santa Anna myself once. He looks like a frog.
This fellow was probably some kind of spy."

They rode back out of the trees into the field. The wind was
blowing stronger now, and the acrid smell of the battle had dissi-

pated in the cool afternoon air. The sunlight glinted on the brass of the six-pounders against the green of the woods where the attack had begun, and a Texian flag was flapping on top of the Mexican breastworks. Toward Vince's Bridge they could see a long column of prisoners being marched back to the Mexican camp. Suddenly, Son realized how thirsty he was, but when he reached for the canteen that had been tied to the back of his saddle he saw that the strap had been cut.

"Take mine," the soldier on the horse's rump said.

Son pulled the wood plug from the canteen and drank until the water poured from his lips.

"You drink like that was whiskey," the soldier said.

The water ran down his chin and neck and over his dusty chest, and as he lifted the canteen higher he thought he could see the whole landscape, the breastworks, the blackened crater where the Mexican cannon had been, the ground strewn with dead men and horses, the violent green of the trees in the distance tilt upward into the shimmering sky, as though it all were being pulled over the earth's edge.

The Texians refused to bury the Mexican dead. Their bodies swelled and blackened under the sun, their distended stomachs bursting the buttons on their uniforms, and at night wild hogs came out of the woods and tore them apart.

On the day after the battle three Texas soldiers chasing a deer found a terrified Mexican in civilian clothes hiding in a canebrake by the bayou. He wept and kissed the hand of the sergeant who captured him and said that he was a private in the army of Santa Anna. When the soldiers took him back to Houston's camp the other Mexican prisoners rose to their feet and began to call out "El presidente." Within minutes a mob of Texians, some carrying coiled ropes, formed around the oak tree where Santa Anna stood shaking before Houston, who lay propped against the tree trunk with his wounded leg held stiffly out in front of him. One man who had escaped execution at Goliad was already tying a hangman's knot in his rope.

But Houston addressed Santa Anna as an equal and had his surgeon give him a piece of opium to hold in his cheek. The language between the two was that of diplomat and negotiator, and Houston even restrained his temper when Santa Anna denied responsibility for the murder of James Fannin and his soldiers at Goliad. The battles, massacres, and burning of towns from Bexar to the San Jacinto River seemed to be slipping away into an abstraction in front of the men who had survived them. As Son and Hugh looked at the muted anger of the other soldiers, dripping weapons in their animal-skin clothes, their wind-burned faces reheated and caught forever with an unsatiated revenge, they felt that a fierce collective spirit even greater than the war it had created to sustain itself was ending here, unfairly, too soon, in the breathless and humid air.

EPILOGUE

It took three months for the new government to begin awarding the promised six hundred and forty acres to each Texas soldier who fought in the war. During that time Son and Hugh shoed horses at a livery stable in Bexar, worked as carpenters, guided a train of German immigrants from Matagorda Bay to the Comal River, and bought a wagonload of whiskey to sell on the Nueces, then lost it the same day when Hugh got drunk in a card game.

Hugh complained about working for wages, the delay in receiving their land, and the presence of German and Polish farmers (he called them "short necks," built low to the ground to do stoop labor that was fit only for Mexican peons and slaves). Son tried to keep him out of the saloons, because the stories they began to hear about San Jacinto had nothing to do with the battle and were told with confidence by men who had not been there, and Hugh would become enraged and offer to fight six men at a time in the street with fists, knives, or axes.

Bexar was changed, too. The soldiers were gone, the Mexican girls sat listlessly in front of the cantina much of the day, the men in deerskin clothes with powder horn and musket were seen less and less, and livestock grazed on the short grass under the scorched walls of the mission. Then they saw the first of a new breed appear in town: the businessman with his carpetbag who spoke not simply of settling and cultivating the land but of the shipping market for vegetables that lay on the coast. And for the first time since they had been together, Son and Hugh were put in jail overnight for disturbing the peace after Hugh threw a chair into a man's face in the saloon. The next morning Hugh threatened the lives of the jailer and the constable who had arrested them, and he was told that if he ever opened his mouth like that again he would be locked away for a month.

Hugh was hung over four days out of the week, and his reputation for drinking on the job and cursing out anyone he didn't like (which was anyone who gave him orders) was so notorious that finally they couldn't get work anywhere. A new saloon that was patronized by land buyers put out a sign for a barkeeper, and when Hugh applied, his clothes stained with horse dung from sleeping in a stable, he was told that he smelled like he had bathed in sheep dip and, secondly, hiring him to barkeep would be like putting an egg-sucking dog in a hen house. The damage to the bar mirror and the owner's nose cost Hugh ten days in jail.

They were broke, and Son was thinking of selling his Kentucky rifle when they received their land deeds in late July. They each were given one-mile-square sections east of the Guadalupe and twenty-five-dollar drafts to buy farm tools and oxen. There was already a settlement of log houses called Yoakum not far from their land, and the newly arrived immigrants had plowed the fields and planted with beans, corn, tomatoes, strawberries, and watermelons. The immigrants were good farmers and worked from first light until after dark, and the earth that had never been turned by a plow was so rich that the seed burst through the top soil with the first rain.

Son and Hugh made a camp on a drainage that wound through their property and cashed their drafts in a farm implement and general store at the settlement. Hugh looked at the prices on the halters, plows, carpenter tools, and square nails, and said, within earshot of the owner, "I ain't buying nothing from these sonsofbitches. It don't cost half this in Bexar."

"That's because I had to haul it from Bexar," the owner said.

"I reckon it gets a lot more valuable bumping up and down in a wagon, don't it?"

"You mean you had me cash your draft and you ain't going to buy nothing?"

Hugh took a tobacco twist out of a jar and put a dime on the counter.

"Start you a new bank with this," he said.

They put their money in their pockets and went next door to the saloon. In the dusty light through the unshuttered windows they drank a quart of whiskey half-empty and watched the immigrant men come in for a single drink and count out their coins carefully from a purse on the bar.

"Look at that one," Hugh said. "Dirt ground into his clothes. Don't speak English. He probably can't count to eleven without using his toes. And how about that head? It looks like it was cut off and glued back on again three inches shorter."

They poured again into their glasses and stared at the dust spinning in the shaft of sunlight through the window. In the distance the clouds looked like black scorches against the blue sky.

"It's too late in the season to grow anything, ain't it?" Son said.

"Hell yes, it is," Hugh said, and threw his saddle bags and then a silver dollar to the black man sweeping the floor. "Go next door and tell that thief to fill it up with jerky and two jars of honey."

They rode north to the Brazos where the Tonkawas had been camped, but the Tonkawas were no longer there. Their conical huts had been burned and lay in ashes on the rings of stone; human and livestock bones were scattered along the river bank, and on a sandbar in the middle of the current there were skeletons still linked together that the coyotes hadn't gotten to. They learned from a buffalo hunter that two months earlier a group of white men had attacked the village before sunlight and had killed almost a hundred people. They shot women with babies, hunted the old ones like mewing animals out of the canebrake, drove the rest into the river and cut them down in a single volley while they stood shaking on the sandbar. The buffalo hunter said the survivors had moved far north on the Brazos.

Son and Hugh followed the river for two weeks. Occasionally, they saw the unshod hoof tracks of Indian ponies or the marks of a travois stenciled deeply in the dried mud, but the signs were old and other Indians besides the Tonkawas were moving north, too. Then at a ford on the river they met some teamsters taking three wagonloads of buffalo hides to Bexar. The teamsters said that the

Tonkawas were living on a drainage three days to the north but often they ran when they saw white men.

When Hugh and Son approached the camp they got off their horses and put their guns on the ground in view of the Indians, who were still too far away to recognize them. There were not more than twenty-five Indians in the camp, and most of them were old people and children. The venison rack over the fire had little meat hanging from it, and the Tonkawas no longer lived in their conical huts but instead in careless lean-tos made from piled brush. The small children, who did not remember Hugh or Son, stayed behind the legs of the older people. Son and Hugh were told that Sana had gone with her cousins to a buffalo hunters' camp up the river to flesh hides for the salted meat the hunters gave them.

They found Sana another day's ride to the north. She was scraping out a hide that was stretched over a willow rack, and the greasy tallow that shaved back from the knife's edge was thick and shiny on her forearms. The hunters' camp reeked of rotted meat. Men stripped to the waist, smelling of sweat and hides, were loading barrels of smoked tongues into a wagon. They hardly paid attention to Son and Hugh until they saw Sana stop her work and stare at them.

"What do you want?" one hunter said. He was breathing deeply from his work, and the black hair on his chest was slick with grease.

"Her," Hugh said.

"That's nice. What else do you want that you can't have?"

"Get up here, Sana. We're going on over the Red," Son said.

"You ain't going nowhere with her, mister."

"You're a dollar-making man, ain't you?" Hugh said. "Been up here putting money in your purse while everybody else was popping caps on the Mexicans. That means you don't tell us nothing."

"There's five of us, walleye. You better pick on another camp if you want to be a squaw man."

"That's just how many balls I got in my Colt. Can you see them loads real good from there?"

Four days later the three of them splashed across the Red River into Indian Territory. The land was flat and baked in the sun, and heat waves seemed to rise off the horizon like distant mountains. The sky was so blue and hard that it looked like it would crack if a rifle ball were fired against it. Their horses' hooves clattered on the rocks in the stillness, and they had to squint their eyes against the white sun's glare to distinguish a tiny clump of oaks from a pool of shadow in an arroyo. Hugh was already talking about a river in Colorado called the Platte and panning float gold as big as elk's teeth. But his description of that country, where he had never been, was not real to Son, because this land here was too immense, like Texas had been, to believe that anything larger could lie beyond it. This land rang under a horse's shoe, it was *now*. The dry rocks in the stream beds had never been cut by a wagon rut, as though the history waiting to happen again had been checked south of the Red River.

Hugh would live out his last years among the Rickaree Indians on the Milk River in Montana, and Son would see war come to Texas again in 1861. His children would ride with General Hood's Texas cavalry at the battle of Atlanta, open the Chisholm Trail from San Antonio to Kansas, and as lawmen bring an end to the Sutton-Taylor feud in DeWitt County. But on that hot day they crossed the Red they didn't think of the power that lay in their blood. They thought only of the dust devils blowing across the plain and the Comanches that could hide like shadows in an arroyo.

All Orion/Phoenix titles are available at your local bookshop or from the following address:

Mail Order Department
Littlehampton Book Services
FREEPOST BR535
Worthing, West Sussex, BN13 3BR
telephone 01903 828503, *facsimile* 01903 828802
e-mail MailOrders@lbsltd.co.uk
(Please ensure that you include full postal address details)

Payment can be made either by credit/debit card (Visa, Mastercard, Access and Switch accepted) or by sending a £ Sterling cheque or postal order made payable to *Littlehampton Book Services*.
DO NOT SEND CASH OR CURRENCY.

Please add the following to cover postage and packing

UK and BFPO:
£1.50 for the first book, and 50p for each additional book to a maximum of £3.50

Overseas and Eire:
£2.50 for the first book plus £1.00 for the second book and 50p for each additional book ordered

---

BLOCK CAPITALS PLEASE

name of cardholder ....

delivery address
(if different from cardholder)

address of cardholder ....

....

....

postcode ....

postcode ....

☐ I enclose my remittance for £...

☐ please debit my Mastercard/Visa/Access/Switch (delete as appropriate)

card number ☐☐☐☐☐☐☐☐☐☐☐☐☐☐☐☐

expiry date ☐☐☐☐   Switch issue no. ☐☐

signature ....

prices and availability are subject to change without notice